Atlantis Lost

Also by T. A. Barron

The Atlantis Saga

Atlantis Rising
Atlantis in Peril
Never Again: The Origin of Grukarr

The Merlin Saga

Merlin: Book One: The Lost Years
Merlin: Book Two: The Seven Songs
Merlin: Book Three: The Raging Fires
Merlin: Book Four: The Mirror of Fate
Merlin: Book Five: A Wizard's Wings
Merlin: Book Six: The Dragon of Avalon
Merlin: Book Seven: Doomraga's Revenge
Merlin: Book Eight: Ultimate Magic
Merlin: Book Nine: The Great Tree of Avalon
Merlin: Book Ten: Shadows on the Stars
Merlin: Book Eleven: The Eternal Flame
Merlin: Book Twelve: The Book of Magic

The Heartlight Saga

Heartlight
The Ancient One
The Merlin Effect

Chapter Book

Tree Girl

Picture Books

Where Is Grandpa?
High as a Hawk
The Day the Stones Walked
Ghost Hands

Inspirational Books

The Hero's Trail
The Wisdom of Merlin

T. A. BARRON

Atlantis Lost

Philomel Books

PHILOMEL BOOKS
an imprint of Penguin Random House LLC
375 Hudson Street, New York, NY 10014

Copyright © 2016 by Thomas A. Barron.
Map of Atlantis illustration copyright © 2013 by Thomas A. Barron.
Map of spirit realm illustration copyright © 2016 by Thomas A. Barron.
Penguin supports copyright. Copyright fuels creativity, encourages diverse voices,
promotes free speech, and creates a vibrant culture. Thank you for buying an authorized
edition of this book and for complying with copyright laws by not reproducing,
scanning, or distributing any part of it in any form without permission. You are
supporting writers and allowing Penguin to continue to publish books for every reader.
Philomel Books is a registered trademark of Penguin Random House LLC.

Library of Congress Cataloging-in-Publication Data
Names: Barron, T. A., author.   Title: Atlantis lost / T. A. Barron.
Description: New York, NY : Philomel Books, [2016] | Series: The Atlantis saga ; 3 |
Sequel to: Atlantis in peril. | Audience: Ages 8–12. | Audience: Grade 4 to 6.
Identifiers: LCCN 2015038985 | ISBN 9780399168055
Subjects: | CYAC: Atlantis (Legendary place)—Fiction. | Fantasy. | BISAC: JUVENILE
FICTION / Fantasy & Magic. | JUVENILE FICTION / Legends, Myths, Fables /
General. | JUVENILE FICTION / Action & Adventure / General.
Classification: LCC PZ7.B27567 Ar 2016 | DDC [Fic]—dc23
LC record available at https://lccn.loc.gov/2015038985
Printed in the United States of America.   ISBN 978-0-399-16805-5
1 3 5 7 9 10 8 6 4 2

Edited by Jill Santopolo. Design by Amy Wu. Text set in 11/16-point ITC Galliard Std.

This is a work of fiction. Names, characters, places, and incidents either are the product
of the author's imagination or are used fictitiously, and any resemblance to actual
persons, living or dead, businesses, companies, events, or locales is entirely coincidental.

----

*Dedicated to
all the places, creatures, and people
where the magic of Atlantis endures*

Contents

Map of Atlantis   x-xi

Map of Spirit Realm   xii-xiii

1. A Gentle Wing   1

2. Rage and Ruin   6

3. Evarra and Noverro   11

4. The Universal Bridge   17

5. A Difficult Choice   22

6. Voice from on High   30

7. The Bridge to Nowhere   35

8. Graybeard   41

9. Magic Circles   48

10. Banana Bread   52

11. Endless Magic with You Goes   58

12. A Dark Passage   67

13. The Crystal Dove   73

14. Swallows   79

15. Searching   84

16. Something to Say   87

17. The Visitors   93

18. Attack   98

19. Plans   *105*

20. Reunited   *114*

21. Anguish   *119*

22. A Well-Deserved Bath   *123*

23. Screams   *127*

24. Collapse   *135*

25. Shangri's Prayer   *140*

26. Our Fight   *146*

27. Faith   *150*

28. Battle for the Spirit Realm   *157*

29. The Flashbolt Cannon   *165*

30. Desperation   *170*

31. The Greatest Single Force   *173*

32. Time to Die   *183*

33. Tidal Wave   *192*

34. One Great Story   *197*

35. The Last Passenger   *204*

36. The Most Magical Place   *207*

Atlantis Lost

CHAPTER 1

A Gentle Wing

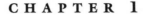

Music had always filled her thoughts—even before she was born.

During all her months in her mother's womb, Omarya heard music everywhere. Songs hummed in her still-forming ears, danced to the cadence of her mother's heartbeat, and flowed through her young veins. None of which was surprising at all, since Omarya was one of the rarest creatures in the spirit realm: a harmonic chimewing.

Youngest in her family—and the first chimewing to be born in many years—her birth inspired a great celebration. Spirit creatures came from all across the realm to sing and dance and play wondrous musical instruments in her honor, crowding around the shimmering silver cloud where her family had lived for eons. The joyful music-making lasted several days . . . and assured Omarya that as rich with song as her time in the womb had been, her new life after birth would be even more sonorous.

In the weeks since, she'd been discovering all the ways she herself could make music. For even though she was a tiny creature—resembling a small butterfly—she possessed the special power of all chimewings: to make music that swelled and flowed out across the spirit realm, reaching countless distant worlds.

All it took to make music, Omarya discovered, was a single beat of her iridescent lavender wings. That simple motion produced the sweeping sound of a dozen violins. (Of course, learning how to play those violins in tune would take years of practice.) Each time she took a breath, the air rang with peals of bells. And the merest twitch of one antenna made a haunting, flutelike sound that echoed eerily for days.

Even better, as a harmonic chimewing, she possessed an additional musical power. She could *think* any sound into reality. All she needed to do was concentrate on whatever she wanted to hear, blink her faceted green eyes, and that very sound would pour out of her head. While this special skill would take time and devotion to master, the possibilities made her little heart flutter with excitement.

Maybe, she told herself, *I could someday become a great bard like my grandfather, invited to perform everywhere.*

At this very moment, Omarya wasn't trying to make music. She was trying, instead, to practice flying. Just a few moments earlier, she'd left her family to take her first solo flight. Though controlling her wings was hard work, she felt increasingly capable.

A sudden gust of wind caught her completely by surprise. She reeled, trying to keep herself upright—but the wind knocked her over, spun her around, and carried her helplessly through the swirling mists. She tumbled out of control as the wind carried her farther and farther away.

Frightened, she made every sound she could, a crashing cacophony of notes and screeches and howls. But the shrieking wind swallowed everything.

Finally, the wind ceased. She found herself floating among dark, shredding clouds, far away from anything she'd ever seen before. The whole region seemed devoid of life, home only to shadows and vapors that felt ominous. Menacing. Frightful.

Omarya couldn't possibly have known that she'd been blown to the remotest edge of the spirit realm. And even if she had known . . . she couldn't have understood the full extent of the dangers.

Desperately, she released a wailing chorus of notes. Though she made the sound of hundreds of bells, ringing and ringing across the skies, they were just one voice. Her voice. The bells echoed, wavering, the cry of someone very young.

Very lost.

Very alone.

A distant flash of color caught her attention. A cloud, bright red, glowed invitingly. Beating her lavender wings, she drew closer.

The cloud, while tattered and thin, looked far friendlier than anything else around. Amidst all the shadows and ghostly vapors, it was truly a welcome sight. Its strange red hue glowed warmly, like a wispy firecoal.

She glided nearer. Just as the very tip of her wing brushed against the cloud—she heard a familiar cry from behind. Her mother!

Omarya whirled around. She and her mother flew tight circles around each other, an aerial embrace that sent elated sounds reverberating throughout the realm. Chimes rang, horns blew triumphantly, and drums pounded with joy.

Together, the pair flew off toward home. So relieved and happy was Omarya that she didn't even glance back for one last look at the luminous cloud. But if she had . . . she would have noticed something strange.

At the instant her wingtip had brushed against the cloud, its light began to fade. Within seconds, the red glow vanished completely. Meanwhile the cloud itself started to shred, pulling apart like an old shawl whose threads had finally given way to time.

The cloud disappeared, its light extinguished forever. But more than just a spot of light had been lost from this faraway edge of the spirit realm. Much more than that had been destroyed.

That luminous cloud was, in fact, part of the great veil woven ages before by Sammelvar and Escholia, the leaders of the spirit realm. The veil's sacred purpose, to separate the mortal and spirit realms, had taken on great importance in the aftermath of the War of Horrors. In that conflict, the warrior spirit Narkazan had brutally attacked the Earth—the necessary first step to conquering all the mortal worlds in the universe. His invasion caused terrible damage to the Earth and its peoples—as well as the immortals who had fought to protect them.

Finally, thanks to the heroic sacrifices of countless beings in both realms, Narkazan was defeated. But his hunger for power continued—and grew stronger with his lust for revenge. For not even a dreadful loss in battle—or a headlong plunge into the Maelstrom from which no one before him had ever escaped—was enough to stop him.

Until now, the only thing that prevented Narkazan from mounting another full-scale attack on the Earth was the veil. Woven from strands of the most powerful magic in the spirit realm, it was designed to shield mortals from another invasion of a large spirit army. And it had done so successfully for many ages.

Yet the veil's makers overlooked a different kind of threat. The barrier wasn't equipped to stop lone individuals, spirits who thought nothing of breaking the law that forbade travel between the realms. Whether they sought the company of someone special in the lands below, or simply craved some tasty food found only on Earth, they discovered holes or made new ones as they passed through, weakening the veil.

Despite Sammelvar's pleas, individual spirits—including his son, Promi—continued to pierce the veil. Finally, the veil grew so weak that only the thinnest strands of remaining magic held it together. Sammelvar had grown so worried about its condition (and so eager to prove the point to Promi) that he illuminated the veil with mist fire, lighting up whatever was left with a reddish glow.

All it took to destroy the veil completely was one last touch from a single being. When Omarya did that, the remaining veil collapsed completely. All the deep magic that had once bound it together dissolved, scattering in all directions.

That was how, in the farthest reaches of the realm, the most powerful barrier ever created was utterly destroyed. Not by an army of warriors . . . but by the lightest brush of a gentle wing.

CHAPTER 2

Rage and Ruin

Narkazan's scream of rage erupted from his lair near the spirit realm's Caverns of Doom. The scream was so loud—and so malicious—that it shattered several enormous icicles hanging from the frozen cloud that hid his lair. Of the icicles that remained intact, many turned a vengeful shade of crimson; others started to drip not water . . . but blood.

His face, narrow as an ax blade, scowled at the pair of mistwraiths who hovered before him. He shook his head, making his battered black earring clink ominously against one of his tusks. As red as those tusks were, they paled next to the fiery centers of his eyes.

"Escape!" he snarled. "You allowed that miserable, meddling son of Sammelvar to break in here—and then escape!"

The mistwraiths trembled fearfully, their

forms quaking like shadows within shadows. That was highly unusual, since normally it was the role of the mistwraiths to make everyone else quake with fright. Everyone, that is, except their brutal master, Narkazan. He knew exactly how to punish them with excruciating pain—and, if he chose, to eliminate them completely.

As the warrior spirit glared at them, both mistwraiths crackled with black sparks. Hovering just above the floor like living blots of darkness, they slid slowly backward until they pressed against the vaporstone wall of the lair. For a long moment, they remained there, held by Narkazan's gaze.

"He even killed one of your company—how, I cannot imagine," Narkazan rasped angrily. "Not only that, he freed my prisoner, his sister the Seer."

He waved a bony hand at the empty room that had served as Jaladay's prison cell. "Her skill at seeing the future would have proved useful in the coming battles."

A low growl came from his throat, echoing in the chamber. "Worst of all, he made off with my scrolls—my battle plans! How," Narkazan demanded, "am I supposed to conduct my War of Glory with those detailed plans now in the hands of my sworn enemy?"

Bravely, one of the mistwraiths slid forward, spraying black sparks on the floor. Though it still trembled with fright, it managed to make a sound that combined harsh crackling and strangled gurgling.

Clearly surprised, Narkazan listened intently. Then, in a much quieter voice, he said, "I suppose you're right. How could I expect you to have stopped him when you weren't even here when he broke in?"

The mistwraith sighed with a shower of sparks. It trembled a little less.

"After all," continued the warlord softly, "you can't be expected to be everywhere at once."

Turning a shade less dark, the mistwraith ceased trembling altogether.

"Except," added Narkazan, his eyes suddenly flashing with rage, "it was your job to protect this place!"

As Narkazan shouted those words, the mistwraith screeched loudly and started to back away again. But before it could join its companion against the wall, the warlord snapped his wrist and hurled a bolt of black lightning. The mistwraith screeched in utter agony, exploded with a spray of sparks, and vanished completely.

All that remained of the dark being were a few last sparks. They quivered, sizzling on the floor. Then they, too, disappeared.

Fixing his gaze on the surviving mistwraith, Narkazan watched it shudder with terror. Finally, he spoke again in the quiet tone that was his most dangerous.

"Never, never, *never* fail me. Or your fate will be the same."

The mistwraith crackled fearfully. Black sparks charred the vaporstone wall.

"Good. Now heed this new command."

Still trembling, the mistwraith did its best to stand at attention.

"Call all the mistwraiths together. Tell them they must divide into two groups—and complete two essential tasks. One group must find that cursed Promi, the son of Sammelvar who bears the mark of the Prophecy on his chest. Yes, find him and bring him to me!"

The growl returned. "I want him alive, do you understand? Not reduced to ashes as you mistwraiths are so fond of doing. No, I want him to suffer through every pain, every torture, I can possibly devise—until he willingly gives up his spirit life forever."

Crackling in assent, the mistwraith bowed.

"And watch out for that buffoon Grukarr, who claims to serve me but keeps botching his tasks. If he ever gets in your way . . ."— he paused to snap his fingers—"destroy him."

The mistwraith gave another bow.

"The other group," rasped Narkazan, "must go to that mortal wasteland Earth. Worry not about the veil, for my scouts have confirmed that it can no longer impede us, no matter how large the force. Somewhere down there is the one thing I want most, the most powerful object in any realm."

He clenched his jaw, hissing as he exhaled through his teeth. "The Starstone. It is hidden on what mortals call Atlantis—the island with so much magic of its own that it conceals the magic of that treasure. Atlantis will be the very first place on Earth I will invade—to take all its natural magic for my own uses. But first I need you to find the Starstone and bring it straight to me."

Glowering at the mistwraith, Narkazan added, "Don't take more than six of your number, for any more than that will trigger the island's power to repel invasions—another of Sammelvar's old curses. But six of you should be more than enough to overpower any foes and find that crystal."

Impatiently, he tapped one of his tusks. "That wretched Promi robbed me once of the chance to turn the Starstone into a weapon—the most destructive one in the universe. He will not do so again!"

Through gritted teeth, the warrior spirit vowed, "And with the corrupted Starstone . . . I shall triumph over all."

Bowing again, the mistwraith crackled eagerly.

With a grim nod, Narkazan announced, "While you warriors do your work, I shall do mine. I will turn my thoughts to two of my servants already in the mortal world. First of all . . . that sea captain turned machinist, Reocoles, will soon have another dream. A truly memorable dream."

He rubbed his pointed chin. "And second, from deep in that rancid pool on Earth's newest island, that place called Atlantis . . . a being will emerge. A monster filled with deep hunger. Yes—the kind of hunger that can be satisfied only by death and destruction."

In a raspy whisper, he added, "And that monster will carry with it something else—something that will make my ultimate conquest of the Earth much easier. Once that is done . . . nothing can stop me from seizing the rest of the universe."

The scars on his face darkened. "That monster could serve another purpose, as well. That fool Promi cares far too much for mortals, proof of his weakness. And the monster from the pool might just bring him out of hiding."

The mistwraith trembled excitedly.

Narkazan strode over to the metal chest beside his cot, the spot where he'd kept the precious scrolls with his battle plans. And then, for the first time in a long while, the malevolent warrior smiled. Though it looked more like a predator baring his teeth, it was for him a real sign of pleasure.

"Now I know," he said aloud, "what to do about those wasted plans."

He nodded with confidence. "If this new idea works . . . it will ensure my victory."

Turning back to the mistwraith, he barked, "Now go!"

Instantly, the shadowy being zipped across the chamber and through the doorway.

CHAPTER 3

Evarra and Noverro

*I*n an entirely different part of the spirit
realm, far away from Narkazan's lair,
five immortals strolled across one of
the realm's grandest creations—the
Universal Bridge. While a vast distance separated them from the warrior spirit's lair, his
goals of conquest weighed very much on their
minds. The group included Promi; his parents,
Sammelvar and Escholia; and his sister, Jaladay
(whose ever-sassy companion, the blue kermuncle Kermi, was riding on her shoulder).

Spanning two of the most populated clusters of worlds in the realm, the Universal
Bridge had been lovingly crafted ages earlier to
connect those places—and to symbolize the
eternal bonds among people everywhere. At
one end of the bridge was a cluster that

constantly radiated a rich array of colors; at the other was a cluster always shrouded in darkness. But the light from the first place was more than enough to make the entire bridge glow and shimmer like the brightest of rainbows, an endlessly luminous archway of shifting colors.

The more radiant end of the bridge rose from one of the spirit realm's most populated galaxies, a collection of worlds called Evarra. Composed of countless bubble worlds, Evarra's planets continually emerged out of the swirling mists, swelled in size even as they transformed in shape and color, vanished suddenly with a *pop*, and then ultimately reappeared from the vapors. Even though, when viewed from the bridge, it might seem that those bubble worlds lasted only a few seconds, time moved differently on the worlds themselves. So in those few seconds, millions of years could have passed on a bubble world.

That cycle of birth, growth, death, and rebirth repeated itself over and over and over again. Given the vast number of worlds in the galaxy, and how rapidly they evolved, anyone who stood on the bridge could hear an endless popping sound—as if the very firmament of the heavens was boiling with the heat of creation.

The group of five paused, leaning on a railing made of reflective vaporstone, to watch the shimmering lights and colors below. After watching in silent contemplation, Sammelvar pushed some locks of white hair off his brow and spoke.

"This view always reminds me how brief our lives really are— winks of light that never last very long. Even we immortal spirits eventually fade away and return to the cosmos. And when we do, whatever we have done with our lives was merely a flash in the ongoing parade of lights."

Escholia, who was standing beside him, placed her delicate, long-fingered hand on his. "What matters most," she said gently, "is not how long our light lasts . . . but how bright it shines."

He nodded, his golden eyes studying her careworn face. "And your light, my dear, shines brighter than anyone I've ever known."

She shook her head humbly. At the same time, though, the ocean-glass crystal she wore around her neck turned a lighter shade of blue, showing that her mood—along with the amulet's sense of the future—had improved.

Modestly, she protested, "That's just because I'm reflecting the light *you* radiate, Sammelvar."

"Not true," he replied. "You've always shined bright. Even all those years ago at our wedding, when I gave you that ocean-glass amulet, you glowed like a star! And now . . ."

He smiled at her, running his hand over one of the bridge's cables that had been studded with prisms to catch the light. "Now you are a whole constellation of stars."

She, too, smiled. The amulet glowed even brighter.

On Sammelvar's other side, Jaladay leaned over the railing. While her eyes remained hidden behind a turquoise band, she could see very clearly the evolving bubble worlds below—more clearly, thanks to her abilities as a Seer, than anyone else. For her vision included glimpses of the past and future of each world and the lives of its people. In fact, she chose to wear the band over her eyes so that she could, in her words, "see without getting distracted by what is too easily visible."

Scanning the array of luminous worlds below, she leaned even farther over the railing. Promi, standing behind her, put his hand on her shoulder and tugged her back toward him. With a chuckle, he said, "Haven't I already saved you once recently? It's too soon to go jumping off a bridge."

"Don't get so cocky, brother. Even if I fell off this thing, I could fly back here without any help from you."

"Not so sure," he objected, shaking his head so that his long black hair swished on his shoulders. "You might get so focused divining the future of some creature down there, you'd forget to fly until you crashed into the planet."

Jaladay almost grinned. "You've got me there. These bubble worlds are just too amazing."

"Harrumph," grumbled the monkeylike creature on her shoulder. "I can blow bubbles, too, you know. Much better ones than those amateurish efforts down there."

Without waiting for her reply, Kermi tapped his long blue tail against Jaladay's back, then released a long breath. More than a dozen blue-tinted bubbles rose from his lips into the air, wobbling as they glistened with sparks of color from the lights of Evarra.

"Not bad," said Promi congenially. "I thought your only real talent was insulting people. Guess I was wrong."

"Guess so, manfool." Kermi's wide blue eyes narrowed. "Which is no surprise, since *your* real talent is getting things wrong."

Refusing to take the bait, Promi said, "That comes from many years of practice."

"Not that many," Jaladay chimed in. "Though you've come awfully close a few times to ending whatever years you've had."

Promi tapped his tunic over the spot where, above his heart, was the black mark of the Prophecy—a bird in flight, wings spread wide. "You have a point there. And I even managed to *die* once, as I recall."

"Some people just can't take a hint," grumbled Kermi.

Sammelvar gazed at his son, an unmistakable look of pride in his expression. "You also found a way to love that most unlovable of beings, a *mistwraith*."

Hearing that word, Jaladay shuddered. Although she'd been safely back with her family for a full day now, she could still feel the cold, destructive power of those shadowy servants of Narkazan. Even the memory of their negative magic seemed to pour darkness into her veins, her lungs, her mind.

Sensing her daughter's distress, Escholia moved to her side. "Are you still feeling the mistwraiths' touch, dear one?"

Jaladay nodded slowly. "As if they still hold me prisoner . . . shrouding me with their darkness." Frowning, she lamented, "I used to enjoy the many degrees of darkness—the shadows, the surprises hidden there. But no longer."

"That's one reason," said Sammelvar, "I wanted us to come here today."

He pointed to the opposite end of the bridge, the side shrouded by night. Completely unlike the wondrous illumination of Evarra's galaxy, the far side of the bridge seemed to be anchored in a place with only one color—totally black. Yet that place, too, was a galaxy in the spirit realm, holding more worlds than could ever be counted.

Noverro. This galaxy of lightless worlds had long intrigued explorers, who had searched for—and found—creatures and civilizations that had evolved in ways enabling them to thrive in the endless night. And Noverro had also long intrigued philosophers, who were compelled by the questions these worlds raised . . . and by the new metaphors they offered. Some argued that enlightenment had a parallel virtue in "endarkenment"; others maintained that understanding shadows could actually be a form of "illumination."

Jaladay peered into the dark galaxy, following the arc of the bridge until it faded into utter blackness. Slowly, she began to notice subtle differences—layers of darkness within darkness, shadows inside shadows. Then, on the shrouded worlds themselves, she sensed the histories and futures of diverse peoples. The high aspirations and deep downfalls of cities. The hopes and fears of individuals.

Observing more closely the bridge where they stood, Jaladay noticed that subtle shadows from the darkened worlds rippled across the prisms and reflective surfaces so full of colors from the lighted worlds. Surprised, she drew a sharp breath. *So the bridge itself is a metaphor,* she thought. *Light and dark completely entwined, each part of the other, each defined as much by what it is as by what it is not.*

"Which is why," said Sammelvar, who had heard her thoughts, "this is called . . ."

"The Universal Bridge," she finished. "Now I really understand."

"Or perhaps," offered her father, "you really see."

CHAPTER 4

The Universal Bridge

A s Jaladay and Sammelvar continued to talk, the Universal Bridge shimmered with colors and shadows. Its great arc, connecting worlds both light and dark, seemed somehow to embrace sunrise, sunset, and midnight all at once.

Escholia listened intently to their conversation, the glow from all the luminous bubble worlds below playing on her white hair. Meanwhile, on Jaladay's shoulder, Kermi remained quiet. Though he wasn't normally someone given to talking philosophy—and would have soundly rejected any suggestion that he might be interested in what he called *existencebabble*—he leaned forward to hear every word.

Promi, however, wasn't listening. Distractedly, he tapped the prisms embedded in one stretch of cable supporting the bridge. With each tap, his thoughts shifted—as if he was giving birth to new ideas as rapidly as the galaxy below was creating new worlds.

Tap. Looking at his mother's face, deeply wrinkled yet just as beautiful and loving as ever, he recalled that people had long ago called her Spirit of Grace.

For good reason, he thought. *That's how she could slip so gently into my dreams during my childhood years among mortals and sing my favorite song. So even while I was banished . . . we were still together.*

Tap. Promi's thoughts shifted to his own dream visit to a mortal—Atlanta, the young woman who'd so unexpectedly captured his attention. And in more recent times, his heart.

But I never told her that! He ground his teeth, frustrated that Atlanta's sentient house, sensing an intruder, had woken her up— right before he could finish the sentence he'd started to say. The sentence he'd finally felt ready to utter: *I really do love you.*

Maybe, he told himself, *I'll get to tell her soon. In person this time.* The idea cheered him, and he drew a deep breath. But as if the shadows from the far end of the bridge had crept into his mind, his thoughts swiftly darkened.

How old will she be then? He knew well that time usually moved slower in the spirit realm than on Earth. (There were exceptions, of course—such as the remote worlds he'd experienced when he and the wind lion, Theosor, had been fleeing Narkazan after stealing the Starstone. In those worlds, time could move very fast, in sudden episodic bursts with no memory between them, or even sideways.) As a result, when he visited Atlanta in her dream, he'd found that what had been just a few weeks for him had been five years for her.

He tapped one of the prisms decisively. *I don't care how much time has passed for her. I'll tell her anyway!* With a swallow, he added, *I just hope she'll want to hear what I have to say.*

Tap. His thoughts suddenly turned to Shangri, the young woman whose carrot-colored hair always wore a dusting of flour from her father's bakery. Shangri's heartfelt prayer, delivered to him by Theosor, had told him that the ship of Greek sailors he'd managed to save from drowning had brought many worrisome changes to Atlantis. Though their leader, Reocoles, called this change "progress," it seemed to Shangri more like destruction. And it also seemed likely to get worse before long.

Glancing down, he saw the familiar bulge in his tunic pocket—the journal Shangri had given him. Like the old one he'd sacrificed to help defeat Narkazan's henchman Grukarr, it was actually a book of recipes. Also like the old one, it had plenty of room in its margins for scribbling journal entries. *Too bad,* he thought sadly, *my life's been moving so fast that I haven't had time to write even a single word.*

Tap. His thoughts turned to Bonlo, his other good friend from Atlantis, and more recently, from their brief encounter in the spirit realm. In both places, Bonlo had saved Promi's life—first, in the terrible dungeon of Ekh Raku, whose stones had been soaked in centuries of blood, where the old monk told him for the first time about the Prophecy that would bring *the end of all magic.* And second, in the sky above a vast ocean, where Bonlo appeared just in time to rescue Promi from the tortures of Grukarr.

He saved my life both times, recalled the young man somberly. *And then I lost him in that ocean, deep underwater where he couldn't possibly survive! After all he'd done for me . . . I couldn't help him when he needed it most.*

Promi heaved a heavy sigh. What made everything worse was

the old monk's unending faith in Promi—faith that Bonlo wore as openly as his white hair. "You may not know it, good lad," he'd been fond of saying, "but you are destined for great deeds."

What's a great deed worth, lamented Promi, *if I can't save the life of a friend?*

Another *tap*—and he thought of another brave friend he'd probably never see again. Ulanoma, the turquoise dragon, had volunteered to distract Narkazan's band of mistwraiths—the same foes who had murdered her mate—to give Promi the chance to rescue Jaladay. As the eldest of all the sea dragons in the spirit realm, Ulanoma was also able to sense the future, both through her own powers and through the ocean-glass crystal she wore as an earring. Yet neither of those could predict whether or not she would survive the mistwraiths.

"What did you think of them, Promi?"

His father's question jolted him back to the present. "What? What did you ask?"

"Harrumph," said Kermi, curling his long tail into the shape of a question mark. "Clueless, as always."

Sammelvar, not amused, restated the question. "I asked you what you thought of Narkazan's battle plans."

Sensing that Promi needed a moment to collect his thoughts, Jaladay commented, "For my part, I was surprised at how detailed they were. But all those details boiled down to one basic idea, the core of his plan: to lure us into a surprise attack—"

"At the Caverns of Doom," finished Promi, sending a grateful glance to his sister. "And it's also clear that he's been assembling a large army."

"Yes," agreed Sammelvar, knitting his brow in concern. "Larger than I would ever have guessed."

"The real question," declared Jaladay, "is what he's going to do now—after we've seen those plans."

"Something different, that's all we can say for sure." Sammel-var ran a hand through his hair. "But *what?*"

No one answered. Silence fell heavily over the bridge. It seemed to Promi that the shadows from the bridge's far end had grown thicker and darker.

Suddenly Jaladay gasped. She wobbled on her feet, then grabbed hold of the railing. Her mother wrapped an arm around her waist for support. Jaladay tilted her head back as if, through her turquoise eye band, she were reading some message scrawled upon the sky.

Which, in a sense, she was—for, as everyone knew, she was having a vision. And by her grim expression, they also knew it wouldn't be a happy one.

CHAPTER 5

A Difficult Choice

Zaladay shuddered, then faced the group. Beads of perspiration rolled down from her forehead onto her eye band. Her skin, paler than usual, seemed to have lost its silvery sheen. Turning her full attention on Promi, she gazed right at him—and from his perspective, right through him.

"The Starstone," she declared. "Narkazan wants to get it back again! He's sent a band of mistwraiths to find it."

"But it's hidden," objected Promi. "Well hidden."

"Yes," his sister countered. She pulled off her eye band and peered at him with eyes as green as a forest at dawn. "It's hidden on *Atlantis*."

Promi winced as if he'd just taken a heavy blow. "And now, thanks mainly to me, there is no more veil to stop them from getting there."

He glanced guiltily at Sammelvar. "I'm so sorry."

The elder man merely placed his hand on Promi's shoulder. Showing no hint of scorn, he said quietly, "You only did what you thought was best at the time."

"But now I know—"

"Now you know more," finished Sammelvar. He added gently, "Like all the rest of us."

Escholia stepped over and looked at Promi with compassion. "This is not your fault. This is Narkazan's fault."

"But," he said sadly, "the veil is destroyed. Gone forever."

"I'm afraid so," agreed Sammelvar. "It took an extraordinary concentration of power to create the veil—so much that I'm not sure we could ever do it again. And even if we tried, we couldn't possibly finish in time to stop Narkazan's plans." His shoulders sagged with the weight of the news. "All that magical energy— once the greatest single force in the spirit realm—is now lost, scattered everywhere."

"Putting the Starstone at risk," said Jaladay with a shake of her head. "As well as Atlantis."

"Especially," added Promi gravely, "Atlanta. She's the only person besides me who knows where it's hidden. And she will guard it with her life."

His mother squeezed his arm but said nothing.

Promi recalled Bonlo's description of the Starstone—the first time Promi had ever heard of it. The old monk's voice had echoed among the dank stone walls of the dungeon as he described it as "a special kind of crystal, capable of magnifying whatever magic is around it. Its very presence makes that magic more powerful— which makes everything more beautiful."

Or, Promi thought, *more dangerous. If Narkazan succeeds at corrupting the crystal, as he's long desired, then he'll have a terrible weapon.*

Jaladay, who had been listening to his thoughts, nodded. "The most terrible weapon in the universe."

Frowning, Sammelvar commented, "If Narkazan finds the Starstone, then both the spirit and mortal realms will be at his mercy."

"Of which he has none," added Escholia.

On Jaladay's shoulder, Kermi's furry ears swiveled anxiously.

"When I was with Atlanta in the Great Forest," said Promi, "a centaur named Haldor made a prediction. A prophecy about Atlantis."

"What did he say?" asked Sammelvar, brushing back his white locks.

Promi gazed over the bridge railing to the luminous, ever-changing worlds below, watching their evolution cast brilliant colors in all directions. Then he turned to the far side of the bridge, where countless worlds lay shrouded in deep shadows. Drawing a long, slow breath, he spoke.

"The centaur warned us that Atlantis, with all its wonders and riches and creatures, would someday perish. He said it would be lost forever, swallowed up by the sea . . . after *a terrible day and night of destruction.*"

Kermi blew a stream of blue-tinted bubbles that rose briefly, then popped and disappeared. "He also said that Atlantis would have a lasting impact on the world. Not from its magic—but from its *stories.*"

"Right," agreed Promi. "He said the tales about Atlantis would survive and grow and be cherished by people all over the world."

"Unless," Kermi pointed out, "that world and others are destroyed by the weaponized Starstone."

"A terrible day and night of destruction," repeated Escholia thoughtfully. "I wonder what that means exactly."

"Something tells me," said Sammelvar, "we'll find out soon enough."

Promi shook his head. "Not necessarily! We all know how prophecies can be misleading."

He touched his chest on the spot where he bore the mark of the Prophecy. "Just remember how baffled everyone was about that line *the end of all magic*. We didn't really know its true meaning until the very last instant before the Prophecy ended."

With more than a hint of gratitude, Jaladay added, "When you figured it out and caused all those miracles."

On her shoulder, the crusty kermuncle grumbled, "The much greater miracle was this dunce figuring out *anything*."

Jaladay gave Kermi a sharp glance, then said quietly to Promi, "Your Prophecy hasn't ended yet. I can feel it. There may be more miracles—and more terrors—yet to come."

She looked at him in that soul-piercing way of hers. "You may not yet know the full meaning of those words, *the end of all magic*."

Though Promi couldn't explain why, he sensed that she was even more upset than she was letting on. As if there was something from her vision that she didn't want to talk about—or even think about. He met her gaze, calling on his power as a Listener to probe deeper. What was she not telling him?

He listened to her heartbeat, her breathing, as well as her thoughts. Beneath all that, he heard the gathering storm of her fears. All at once, he understood.

"You know something else about Atlantis, don't you?" he asked quietly. "Something you know will upset me?"

Jaladay's eyes narrowed. "Curse that Listener magic of yours!"

"Hmmm, are you forgetting who gave it to me?"

"A mistake I now regret."

Kermi thumped his tail against her back. "Don't say I didn't warn you."

"You did," she said with a sigh. Then, gazing at her brother, she explained, "Once Narkazan gets the Starstone, he will use it to destroy any opposition to him in the spirit realm."

"Starting with us," said Escholia.

Sammelvar nodded grimly.

"Then," continued Jaladay, "he will move to invade Earth, since that's the best way to conquer the entire mortal realm."

"What else did you see?" asked Promi, sure there was more.

She lowered her voice. "The first place on Earth he will go— the very first stop—will be Atlantis. He wants to seize all its natural magic—every last bit of it."

Promi shuddered. "So Atlantis will be just a source of fuel for his weapons—including the Starstone."

She reached out and touched his arm. "I'm sorry, Promi. The last thing you wanted when you sacrificed so much to create that island was that it would . . ."

"Become Narkazan's favorite target," he grumbled. "And I even put Atlantis in a spot in the ocean all by itself where he'd have no trouble finding it."

"You couldn't have known, son," said Sammelvar gently.

"Maybe," added Escholia, trying to sound more hopeful than she felt, "there is still a way to stop Nark—"

Whooshhhhh. A sudden rush of air swept over them, cutting her off. Everyone on the bridge knew instantly that it hadn't come from any gust of wind. No, it came from an arriving wind lion.

"Theosor," said Promi, suddenly feeling a little better. Despite all the dire news and troubling prophecies, it always lifted his spirits to see the majestic creature who had carried him to his first quest in the spirit realm.

"Hello, young cub." Theosor's richly toned bass voice rolled across the bridge as he banked in the mist above Promi and the others. As always, there was a constant vibration above the lion's muscular torso—but no visible wings. Theosor's huge forepaws swept through the air, while a breeze tousled his silver-hued mane.

With a bow, the wind lion rumbled, "Greetings to you, Sammelvar and Escholia, Jaladay and Kermi—and you, as well, Prometheus."

"And ours to you, Theosor," answered Sammelvar in the traditional style. "What news do you bring?"

Theosor probed them with his great brown eyes, then said, "Nothing good."

Sammelvar drew closer, leaning against the railing of the bridge. "Tell us."

"Mistwraiths," the wind lion began, saying the word with distaste as if he'd swallowed a rotting carcass. "A band of them was seen just moments ago, flying to the Earth. They seem to be heading—"

He paused, glancing at Promi before finishing the sentence. "To Atlantis. Clearly, Narkazan sent them there on some sort of mission."

"To regain the Starstone," declared Jaladay. She slipped the turquoise band back over her eyes. "I saw it just now in a vision."

Theosor, hovering in the air on the other side of the railing, released a deep growl. "I feared as much."

"And if he gets it," continued Jaladay, "he'll waste no time corrupting it into a weapon."

"A terrible weapon that threatens both the spirit and mortal realms," said Sammelvar somberly.

Theosor nodded, his mane fluttering. "There is more. My scouts tell me that Narkazan himself is amassing a huge army—but not at the Caverns of Doom, as he originally planned."

Promi and Jaladay traded glances, knowing that they had spoiled the warlord's original plans by stealing his scrolls.

"So," pressed Sammelvar, "exactly where are they gathering?"

"I still need to confirm that. But it seems to be far past the Caverns, in the region of Xarnagg."

"One of the remotest places in the realm," said Sammelvar with a scowl. "We need confirmation soon, if we are going to mount an attack before Narkazan gets his hands on the Starstone."

Theosor hovered closer. "I am going to do that now." He glanced over at Promi. "Would you care to join me on another quest, young cub? The whole realm depends on us . . . just like old times."

Torn, Promi shifted his weight uneasily. He looked from the wind lion to his parents, then to Jaladay and Kermi—all of whom were watching him. "I . . . I don't know," he said hesitantly. "Half of me wants to go with you . . . but the other half wants to head for—"

"Atlantis," finished Jaladay. "Of course. The Starstone is there—and so is Atlanta. This is a difficult choice."

"You're telling me," he muttered.

"Well, young cub," Theosor rumbled, "you must decide."

Escholia took Promi's hand, and said gently, "Go where your heart leads you."

"But," he protested, "it's leading me in two separate directions."

"Time is short," the wind lion rumbled.

"Whatever you choose," said Sammelvar, "we trust your judgment." Locking gazes with Promi, he added, "You have earned that trust, my son."

Promi took a deep breath, filling his lungs with the misty air of the spirit realm. "I will go to Atlantis. To stop them from getting the Starstone."

"So be it," declared Theosor. "Stay in one piece, young cub."

"I will if you will," Promi replied.

Another whoosh of air—and the wind lion reared back on his powerful hind legs and vaulted into the sky.

His face lined with concern, Sammelvar cautioned Promi, "The skill you showed while rescuing Jaladay, stopping a mistwraith with love, will only work on one of those beings at a time. Not if you are faced with a whole band of them."

Jaladay shivered at the thought.

"I know," the young man replied. "But I must do whatever it takes to stop them. For the sake of us all."

"Then go, son." Sammelvar gazed at Promi for a long moment. "You take with you our love . . . as well as our hopes."

CHAPTER 6

Voice from on High

Evening had come to Atlantis. And Reocoles, master machinist, had fallen asleep at his worktable.

After an arduous day's work, none of that night's noises were enough to wake him. Not the creaking and grinding of machinery in his workshop, nor the heaving of the huge bellows that heated his furnace for melting metals, nor the constant din of vehicles on the streets of the City of Great Powers—vehicles he had invented, whose coal-powered motors kept chugging past all through the night. Still wearing his work apron, smudged with grease, he slumbered.

But not well. He shifted in his chair, nearly falling out of it completely. His head, resting on his arm atop the worktable, turned constantly. Even his weak leg with its brace kept twisting, knocking against one leg of the table.

Right behind him stood the captain's wheel from his wrecked ship, the only piece of the boat he'd been able to salvage from the wreckage. He'd carried it here to his factory in the City and mounted it in his workshop where he could see it every single day. To remind him of that moment when he and his crew had been saved by Poseidon, the Greek god of the sea—who had, he felt sure, sent a gigantic wave in the shape of a watery whale's tail. That wave had rescued the doomed ship and cast it ashore on Atlantis, a true miracle. A miracle from the gods.

Reocoles would not have believed that the wave had actually been brought by an ancient sea goddess who had heard a heartfelt plea from Promi. The only mortal who knew the truth of what had happened on that day was Shangri, the baker's daughter.

For over five years now, the old wooden wheel had sat in this workshop—the only unchanging fixture as Reocoles's many inventions and raw materials had piled up around the cavernous room. The wheel, whose knobs still glistened with flecks of white sea salt, bore a chipped brass plate the master machinist had inscribed with the motto that had guided him ever since the day he set sail from Greece: *the Control of Nature.*

That motto, Reocoles believed, embodied the greatest gifts of mankind—gifts that separated humans from the rest of the animals and brought them closest to the gods. Cleverness, ingenuity, and persistence. And Reocoles knew in his heart that one of those gods had taken a special interest in his own life. Hephaestus, god of all crafts and machines, must surely have known that this mortal man—like the god who inspired him—possessed a relentless drive to conquer and exploit nature for the benefit of his people. As well as the profit it could bring him.

As Reocoles slept on this particular night, he dreamed that the old ship's wheel suddenly came to life. With a loud *snap*, it flew off its mount—and into his eager hands. The magical wheel then carried him right out the door and high into the sky.

Below, Reocoles could see the whole City he'd successfully improved so much in the past five years. Oil-burning lamps lit the street corners that once were dark at night. Their light helped to catch some of the criminals who had for some reason multiplied since he'd started to industrialize the region. Soon, he knew, those lamps would be replaced by the modern gas lamps he'd been developing in his laboratory. Vehicles, pouring coal dust from their smokestacks, carried workers and supplies even at this late hour. Pipes full of water ran along the rooftops. With a satisfied grin, Reocoles spied the special water system he'd recently installed on the roof of the Divine Monk's temple.

As long as that monk gets his hot bath in the evening and fresh food four or five times a day, thought Reocoles, *I can always count on his support.*

As his chest swelled with pride, the master machinist suddenly heard a powerful voice from the heavens. That voice, he felt certain, belonged to none other than the great god Zeus.

"Hear me, you miserable mortal," boomed the god. "You heeded my first command and have started to remake this city and this island. That command set you on the road to gaining all the power you *might* have deserved."

"I owe it all," he said modestly, "to the guidance I've received from you, Great One, and Hephaestus."

Satisfaction swept through Reocoles. And yet . . . something troubled him about how the god had said the word *might*.

Abruptly, the wheel turned and tore Reocoles away from the gleaming city. He flew, without any ability to steer, over the Divine Monk's ornate quarters, past the city gates, across the deep chasm of the Deg Boesi River, and above the dark expanse of the Great

Forest. Peering into the empty blackness below, Reocoles felt a stab of pain that his extensive mining operations at the edge of the forest had recently halted—all because of a meddling forest girl named Atlanta.

"Then why," accused Zeus, his voice echoing among the clouds, "have you failed me? Why have you abandoned the road to triumph?"

Before Reocoles could offer even a meek reply, the entire vista changed dramatically. Daylight flooded the isle of Atlantis, revealing the complete forest, an untamed swath of greenery. Beyond, in the distance, lay wide, grassy meadows and a mysterious, spiral-shaped bay. None of those lands showed any signs of human development, though Reocoles had long hoped to change that.

Directly below him lay the open pit mines, refinery operation, and huge vehicles of his industrial complex—all of them now abandoned and silent. The only movement came from the large waste pool, dismal yellow in color, which bubbled continuously. Perhaps, from the depths of the pool, something else stirred . . . but Reocoles couldn't be certain.

"If you do not do as I have commanded," roared the god, "all your works shall vanish. Behold!"

Reocoles, holding the flying wheel more tightly than ever, gasped. An enormous wave, many times larger than the watery whale's tail that had rescued his ship, rose out of the sea. Racing toward the island, it smashed into the cliffs and swept across the City of Great Powers. Buildings, temples, homes, vehicles, and bridges all disappeared under the titanic wave. Reocoles's factory and all his equipment and inventions vanished in a few brief seconds. Not even a cloud of dust from the wreckage remained, for the sea had swallowed everything.

"Great god," pleaded the master machinist, "give me another

chance, I beg of you. I shall satisfy your command of progress, whatever that requires!"

From the clouds came only a distant rumble, like a faraway growl. "You must, in addition, do one thing more."

"Tell me, Zeus. Please."

"You must stay ever vigilant against the enemies of your work! For there are individuals who would see you and all your achievements destroyed."

Thinking of that troublesome forest girl, Reocoles answered, "Worry not about her! I have already made plans that will completely stop her meddlesome ways."

"Waste no more efforts on her, then. The one individual you must guard most against—the one who is your greatest nemesis— is a young man who calls himself Promi. You will recognize him by the black mark of a bird in flight on his chest."

Nodding anxiously, the machinist promised, "I shall find him, Great One. And I shall destroy him!"

"Heed my words. You cannot destroy him by yourself. He is too powerful. You must capture him and deliver him to my immortal servants, warriors of darkness who will seem to you only a mass of shadows."

The voice grew louder. "Do you understand?"

"Y-yes, yes, I do."

"Good! Now get back to work, you wretched mortal. Prove your worth to me and . . . you shall thrive. *Fail me and . . .*"

As the voice from on high paused, Reocoles shuddered. His sweaty hands grasped the flying wheel, high above the endless ocean where once Atlantis had flourished. Nervously, he awaited the god's final words. When at last they came, they smote the sky like terrible thunder.

"You shall perish forever."

CHAPTER 7

The Bridge to Nowhere

At the same time that Reocoles, in another part of the City, dreamed of his encounter with the all-powerful god, two young people strolled together down a cobblestone street. Lit by the flickering light of oil lamps, the stones under their feet gleamed subtly, like stars through rising mist.

"I jest can't forget," said Shangri sadly, "the first sight o' that mining operation. It was a week ago now, but it feels like jest a few seconds. Giant pits, hills stripped o' every last tree, an' those huge wagons belchin' smoke an' tearin' away at the ground. Plus that horrible yellow pond where Reocoles's soldiers tried drownin' me."

She frowned at her companion, Lorno. He

looked at her with real compassion, crinkling his nose in that special way of his. "Sure glad Atlanta came in time to save you!"

Shangri nodded, bouncing her long red hair. "Atlanta an' her faeries." Her frown melted. "Ye should have seen them, little as they were, attackin' all the soldiers."

"Maybe someday I'll write about that battle."

"Or somethin' better," said Shangri with a playful wink. "Like that *one great story* yer still searchin' to find."

Lorno gave her a look of determination. "I *will* find it, Shangri."

"I know ye will." She took his hand. "It will be a story the world will never forget."

They stopped walking at the intersection with the wide avenue that ran along the edge of the river's deep gorge. Far below the rim, water crashed and pounded ceaselessly.

Looking at each other, their eyes glistened, maybe from something more than the street lamps. Despite her playful tease, Shangri loved Lorno's high aspirations. Through all five years she'd known him, his dream of becoming a famous bard had remained as strong as ever. As strong as it had been on the first day they'd met—the day Promi had caused that great watery whale's tail to rise out of the sea and save Lorno's ship.

Of course, as Shangri knew well, it hadn't really been Lorno's ship. The vessel belonged to Reocoles, and Lorno was merely a lowly crew member, the apprentice to the assistant deck-mopper. But in the time since the shipwreck—when he'd landed right on top of Shangri's father, the baker Morey—Lorno had become her best friend . . . and something much more than a friend.

Several months earlier, they'd been married by an old monk at the temple. Seeing the young couple's delight at being wed, the monk had given them a wondrous ceremony, sprinkling colorful flower petals over them and chanting many blessings to bring them good fortune. The monk had even refused to take any payment—until, that is, Shangri's father had offered him a freshly baked plum pie, still steaming hot from the oven. No one could resist that.

"The City has changed a lot since ye first came here," she said softly to Lorno. "Yet despite all the ways we both wish it hadn't . . ."

She paused to glance at a pile of discarded machine parts and packaging that someone had dumped on the street corner. "Despite all those ways, I sure am glad fer one special change."

Lorno grinned, squeezing her hand. "I'm glad for that too."

"So is Papa." She returned the young man's grin. "At least since his back healed from yer landin' on top o' him."

"Right. I must have weighed almost as much as one of his triple-deep cherry pies."

Shangri chuckled. "Not quite that much, thank the Divine Monk's bountiful beard."

"You mean his bountiful *belly*," corrected Lorno mischievously. "That's the most bountiful part of him. Except maybe all his many chins."

"Shhh," cautioned Shangri—though she couldn't keep herself from laughing out loud, even as a trio of monks turned the corner and walked past. The monks, wearing brown robes and sandals, chanted in worshipful monotones as they padded down the street. They marched in unison, stepping in time to the small prayer drum one of them struck rhythmically.

As the monks turned another corner and disappeared, Lorno said, "Back to the subject of my writing—"

"Ye mean yer paper crumplin'," teased Shangri. "Last time I looked in yer room, there were more crumpled pages than anythin' else, takin' up more space than yer bed."

"I know," he said, lowering his gaze. "The writing hasn't been going well." Suddenly brightening, he said, "But I do have a new writer's name."

She rolled her eyes. "What, again? I gave up countin' how many names you've tried."

"Which is why you still call me Lorno, the name I had when we first met."

"An' the name fer ye I told the monk who married us," she remembered with a chuckle.

"So you really do like that name?" he asked.

Shangri sighed. "Well . . . no, to tell the truth. But if I didn't keep callin' ye that, I'd totally lose track o' yer name!"

"Well," he began hopefully, "how about this new name I just thought of this afternoon?"

"An' it is?"

"It is . . ." His voice trailed off, and his expression darkened. "Zeus's thunderbolt! I, well—I um . . . forgot it."

Shangri stifled another laugh. "Guess it wasn't goin' to last anyway."

"Nothing I've created yet is going to last," he said in a forlorn voice.

She gave him a sympathetic hug. "Ye'll find yer true name. Jest like ye'll find yer one great story."

"You think so?" he asked hopefully. "A story that will reach across time and distance, touching people everywhere?"

"Yes. Yer one great story." Then, whispering in his ear, she added, "But whatever yer name as a famous bard . . . to me, ye'll always be Lorno."

He nodded gratefully, then whispered, "And to me . . . you'll always be a prayer that was answered."

She caught her breath. "Speakin' o' prayers—oh, Lorno! Last night, jest before I fell asleep, I heard *a voice* inside my head. Promi's voice!"

"Are you sure?"

"As sure as there's plenty o' freckles on my face."

"Well," he said wryly, "that's very sure." But seeing that she was now in no mood for humor, he pressed, "What did he say?"

Shangri concentrated, calling back the whole memory. "He said he got the prayer I sent him from the old bridge that's fallin' apart."

She pointed to the river gorge where the barest outline of the dilapidated, half-finished bridge could be seen. The Bridge to Nowhere, Promi had called it. Mist, rising from the thundering river below, billowed all around. From every plank and post, lines of silver leaves inscribed with prayers fluttered in the breeze.

Lorno crinkled his nose in doubt. "So the old legends are true?"

"Yes! I'm sure o' that now. He said my prayer came to him on a wind lion, jest like the legends say. An' then he told me what I needed to hear."

"Which was?"

Shangri swallowed. "In my prayer to him, I told him about Reocoles an' the mines. An' all the troubles we're now havin' on this island."

Again Lorno asked, "What did he say?"

Her steady gaze bore into him. "That he'll never abandon us. *Never.* An' that . . . he still loves Atlanta. Even if they can't ever be together."

Lorno blew a long breath. "Being immortal isn't all that easy, I suppose."

"Not," added Shangri, "when the one person you most want to be with is livin' on another world."

His voice very quiet, Lorno said, "I'm glad we're living on the same world."

"Me too." Her face seemed to harden. "But we can't wait for Promi to come back an' help us. We've got to do somethin' *ourselves* to stop Reocoles."

"You already did that," objected Lorno. "Even though you almost got yourself killed in the process."

Shangri shook her head vigorously, sending up a puff of flour from that day's long hours in the bakery. "Atlanta an' I—we only stopped him fer the moment! He's already put out the call fer more workers. Offerin' them twice the old wages. Plus a bonus fer startin' right away."

"Are you sure about that?"

"Sure as can be. Heard lots o' folks talkin' about it at the bakery today, while ye were up in yer room, writin' away."

"Crumpling away," he said morosely.

Lorno scanned the avenue by the river, where several abandoned vehicles cluttered the rim of the gorge. Furtively, people were even now looking the vehicles over, searching for any objects they could sell. Despite their common purpose, none of those people spoke to one another, or even nodded in greeting as they would have done just a few years ago.

"You know," he observed, "all those inventions and machines that Reocoles has made for the City do some useful things. Convenient things. But they also hide a lot of troubles—and those troubles are spreading, like a disease."

"Which is why," Shangri declared, "we're goin' to do somethin' about it."

"What?"

"I'm not sure yet." She tugged on his arm, spun him around, and started to walk back up the cobblestone street. "But by the time we get back to the bakery, I'm hopin' to know."

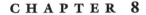

CHAPTER 8

Graybeard

Yer plannin' to do *what?*"

Morey the baker roared at his daughter, his round face as red as a strawberry tart. Facing Shangri and Lorno at the back of his bakery, he glared at them, his mouth open as wide as one of his ovens.

"I told you, Papa. We need to stop him! Before it's too late."

Morey planted his fists on his ample hips, smearing on his apron some of the cherry pudding he'd just been stirring. That hardly mattered, though, for the apron already wore everything from raspberry syrup to flecks of dough to sprinklings of flour—signs of a typical day's work.

"I won't hear of it!" he bellowed, this time loud enough that he startled the three or four evening customers on the other side of the counter.

Although those customers had come to the bakery as their last errand of the day, hoping to gather some pastries before the shop closed, they immediately changed their minds and went straight home. Only one person remained on that side of the counter—a tall, gray-bearded man wearing a ragged old coat. Even as the man studied the pastries on display on the shelves, his dark eyes glanced furtively at the people in the back.

Seeing the red-haired girl, the young man beside her, and the plump baker, the man grinned knowingly, as if the three of them fit some description he'd been given. Surreptitiously, he took another look at Shangri, watching her closely. Then his grin broadened.

Meanwhile, trying his best to stay calm, the baker said to Shangri, "Tell me again this crazy-brained idea o' yers. I thought ye'd just gone out for an evenin' walk, the two o' ye. An' then ye come back here plottin' a bloody revolution!"

On the other side of the counter, the bearded man raised an eyebrow.

Shangri stepped closer to her father and gently touched the apron that wrapped around his wide waist. Under that colorfully stained apron, she could feel the bulge of his belt buckle—which was, as she knew well, the sapphire-studded buckle that Promi had stolen from the wicked priest Grukarr and then given to her father.

Promi had called that generous gift "a small payment" for one of the baker's sweet and gooey cinnamon buns. Its valuable jewels had freed Morey from needing to bake for a living. So why did he continue to run the bakery, getting up every morning two hours before dawn to start preparing the day's treats and working until late every evening? *Fer the simple pleasure o' doin' it,* he would answer. And Shangri knew that, for him, that pleasure came mainly from seeing others enjoy his baked goods.

"Listen, Papa," she said softly, "ye know what happened to me when I went to see Reocoles's mines across the gorge."

"I do indeed!" he thundered. "An' it made me want to pummel that evil man like a big mound o' dough."

Morey punched the air vigorously to illustrate the point. "An' then I'd slice him into pieces like one o' me pies."

"I know, Papa, I know. It's only because I made ye promise not to do it that he's still alive."

"Right, dumplin'." He sighed. "An' it's only thanks to that brave young woman from the forest that *yer* still alive. I owe her a mountain o' me best pastries, I do! What was her name again?"

"Atlanta."

Across the bakery, the bearded man leaned over the counter to listen.

"An' yer right, Papa. I'm only here today because o' her."

Ruffling her carrot-colored hair with one of his hands, Morey asked, "So why do ye want to put yerself in danger *again*? Yer dealin's with that hooligan will only make ye more likely to get hurt. Or worse."

He peered into her eyes. "An' dumplin' . . . I jest couldn't survive that."

Shangri glanced over at Lorno, who frowned, and said, "He has a good point, you know."

"Ye bet yer last drop o' cookie dough, I do!"

"O' course, Papa." Shangri bit her lip. "But if we can stop Reocoles now—before he gets that whole minin' operation started again—we jest might stop him *forever*."

"But how," her father demanded, "could ye possibly do that? Short o' bloody revolution, I don't see how ye can hope to succeed."

He paused, grimacing. "I'm not saying there aren't plenty o' folks feelin' angry about him an' his cursed machines. But

dumplin' . . . ye won't be able to find enough people who'd be wil-
lin' to risk life an' limb fer that cause. There's jest too many folks
needin' Reocoles's money—or his water fer their homes."

"Exactly as he planned," said Lorno.

"I know that," declared Shangri. "An' that's why I've thought
of a *different* way to stop him. One that doesn't need any help from
folks here in the City."

Now the bearded man slipped around the counter, stepping
quietly toward the back of the bakery, to make sure he didn't miss
a single word.

"Tell us, dumplin'."

"All I need to do," Shangri explained, "is go into the Great
Forest an' talk with Atlanta. *She'll* understand! An' I'm sure that
she could convince the forest creatures to help! Why, with enough
faeries an' bears an' monkeys an' others, it'll be as good as a regu-
lar army!"

Morey rubbed his forehead, knocking loose a clump of dough.
"Ye know . . . that really could work, seein' how effective jest the
faeries were last time."

"That's right," Shangri said with a bright smile. "Atlanta knows
all those creatures. An' they trust her."

"Only one problem," Lorno observed. "How do you *find*
Atlanta? The forest is almost impassable unless you know one of
the trails—and I don't think you do. On top of that . . . you don't
know where in that huge forest to find her! You could end up wandering around in the woods, totally lost, to the end of your days."

Shangri straightened her back. "That won't happen to me."

"Why not?" demanded Morey and Lorno in unison.

"Because," she announced, "I have *this*."

As her father and husband watched, she drew from her pocket
a small green bundle that looked like a crumpled leaf. Holding it
in the palm of her hand, she said, "Open now."

Instantly, the leaf unfurled, flattening out on Shangri's hand. Shaped like a circle with deep indentations around the edges that looked almost like fingers, the leaf actually resembled a flattened green hand. In its center lifted a thin red shoot, clasping a tiny piece of honey-colored amber that narrowed to a sharp point.

"Beautiful," said Morey. "Nature really is the best artist—an' also the best baker."

Still puzzled, Lorno asked, "How does this help?"

"Watch," said Shangri. Then she commanded, "Show me the way."

Right away, the piece of amber started to spin, turning rapid circles. Suddenly, it stopped, its point facing the bakery's door to the street.

Morey gasped. "It's a compass! A magical compass. How, dumplin', did ye ever get such a treasure?"

"From Atlanta, jest before we parted. She told me to use it if I ever wanted to find her again."

"That's fantastic," said Lorno.

"Amazin'," added Morey.

"Most helpful," said a melodic voice that none of the others had ever heard before.

Shangri, along with Morey and Lorno, spun around to face the source of the voice—the man with the gray beard. He had crept so quietly across the bakery that nobody had noticed him.

Morey drew himself up to his full height and rumbled, "Who are ye? This part o' the bakery is jest fer me an' my family."

"So sorry to disturb you," the man said apologetically. He gave the baker a twinkling smile, then bowed low.

As he straightened up again, the man said in his lilting, melodic voice, "I am honored to meet you." Something about his voice felt calming—almost hypnotic—so that whatever he said, people felt inclined to agree with him.

"Are ye here fer a pastry?" asked Morey, speaking more calmly now . . . yet still with an edge of suspicion. "If so, me goods are there on the counter. Yer welcome to take whatever ye'd like fer free. But then ye should go, since it's past closin' time."

The man smiled again and said pleasantly, "The truth is, I did come here hoping to buy a pastry or two. But as I stood at your counter . . . I just couldn't help overhearing your plans."

Shangri, like the others, stiffened. "What plans?"

"Clever girl," said the man mellifluously. "Your plans to stop that wicked man Reocoles, once and for all." His voice took on a harder edge as he vowed, "I want to help you defeat him. It's a true crime what he's done to our fair City of Great Powers."

Shangri breathed a sigh of relief. "We could always use more help."

"Slow down, dumplin'." The baker scrutinized the stranger. "Ye seem very nice, a real gentleman. But even so . . . we don't know you from a pecan tart. So how are we s'posed to trust you?"

"Good question, Master Baker." His voice as sweet as the honey-eyed syrup Morey liked to drizzle over pastries, the man explained, "I give you my word that I hate that horrible man as much as any of you. Possibly more."

Despite his initial doubts, Morey nodded. How could he ever have doubted such a good, honest fellow?

Seeing that he'd won the baker's confidence, the man continued, "And I do have certain skills that might prove helpful."

"What skills?" asked Morey.

"Could ye show us?" Shangri asked.

With a nod, the man opened his coat, revealing a row of knives inside. "I'm a traveling performer," he explained. "What I do to entertain people is . . ."

With a lightning fast movement, he whipped out a knife and

hurled it at the wall. The blade sank deep into the wood, leaving the handle quivering from the impact.

"That's fine," said Lorno. "But I can do that too. It's not that special."

The man raised an eyebrow. "Then what do you think of this?"

Instantly, he threw two more knives, one after the next. One buried its blade in the very top of the first knife's handle. And the other buried itself in the handle of *that* knife. All three knives protruded from the wall, trembling like a long branch that had just sprouted there.

"Well now," said Lorno approvingly. "That really *is* impressive."

Turning to Shangri, the stranger asked with sincere politeness, "Would you allow a lowly entertainer, a humble knife thrower, to join your company?"

Shangri nodded. "Oh, yes, I surely would. Yer throwin' skills could be very useful." Turning to her father, she asked, "Don't ye agree, Papa?"

Morey nodded, as well. Then, facing the stranger, he asked, "Would ye swear to do whatever it takes to keep me daughter here safe?"

The man said decisively. "I would."

"Even if that means hurlin' one o' yer knives at some attacker?"

"Even if it meant throwing *all* my knives at a whole army of attackers."

Morey grinned. Extending his meaty hand, he said, "Welcome, then. Ye can call me Morey."

The man smiled with satisfaction and extended his own, much slimmer hand. "And you can call me Graybeard."

CHAPTER 9

Magic Circles

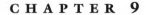

"All right, then," announced Shangri. She carefully placed the leaf compass in her pocket, then gazed at her companions in the bakery. "Let's meet here again at sunrise; then we'll be leavin' fer the forest."

"At sunrise," repeated Graybeard. His dark eyes gleamed. "I'm looking forward to it."

With that, he turned and stepped away silently. Crossing the bakery, he passed the counter and grabbed a plump blackberry tart. With a wink at Morey, he breezed out the door and disappeared.

"Such a nice fellow," the baker said, watching Graybeard go.

"And," added Lorno with a grin, "he has great taste in pastries."

Morey chuckled, then gently elbowed his daughter. "Jest like yer old friend Promi."

Shangri nodded, bouncing her red locks. "But there's a thumpin' big difference between the two o' them. As much skill as he has as a knife thrower, he can't do anythin' as wonderful as Promi."

"That's true," agreed the baker. "I'm so glad ye finally told me Promi's big secret—that he's really an immortal. That explains a lot! Never has a pie thief had so much amazin' magic."

"You're right about that!" exclaimed Lorno. "His magic caused the wave that gave me . . ." Pausing, he eyed Shangri with affection. "A whole new life."

Morey smirked, then added, "That wave gave me somethin' too."

"What, Papa?"

"A mighty sore back!" He burst out laughing, making his prominent belly shake like a mound of lemon custard.

The others joined in, filling the bakery with laughter. As Shangri and Lorno quieted again, Morey told them, "It sure tickles me heart to see the two o' ye so close these days. Ever since ye got married . . . ye've looked so happy together."

The baker nodded, then said wistfully, "Seein' ye two reminds me—well . . . never mind." He shook his head, embarrassed. "It's none o' me cracklin' business."

Shangri looked at him lovingly. "What is it, Papa? Ye can tell us."

"Well, sweetcake . . ." He shook his head again. "Really, I shouldn't say. It's yer life, not mine."

"Please, Papa?" She smiled at him. "We'd really like to know."

He blew a big sigh. "Well . . . it's jest that, lass . . . ye remind me so much o' yer ma." Blinking the mist from his eyes, he whispered, "When I first met her, she looked so much like ye do right now."

Her own eyes misty, Shangri said nothing.

"An' when I watch ye two together," the baker went on, "it reminds me o' those blessed days. Everywhere we went, yer ma an' me, it seemed like we were standin' inside a magic circle."

Taking hold of his meaty hand, Shangri replied, "That's jest how it feels to us, Papa."

"Every day," declared Lorno, moving to her side.

Morey nodded. Reaching out his burly arms, he embraced the two of them. "Now ye have yer own magic circle."

"Yes, Papa. We do."

Struck by a sudden inspiration, the baker released them. "Wait here," he said. "Jest fer a moment."

Quickly, he darted to the counter at the front of the bakery and grabbed something from one of the shelves. Then he searched through several drawers, hurriedly slamming one and opening the next as he searched. At last, holding some objects against his apron, he hustled back to Shangri and Lorno.

As he approached them, he extended his hand, which held a lone cinnamon bun. Though it looked a bit stale after sitting most of the day on a shelf, it still smelled wondrously sweet. With an unmistakable look of satisfaction, Morey handed it to the young couple.

"There," he announced. "Another wedding cake. Jest to continue yer celebratin'! It's not so special as the one I baked fer ye on the day ye got married, but it's—"

"Still wonderful!" cried Shangri joyfully. Bringing the pastry to her face, she inhaled its sweet aroma of cinnamon, butter, and sugar. "If Promi could be here, he'd agree."

"You can tell him someday," said Lorno.

As swiftly as a cloud hides the sun, Shangri's expression darkened. "I hope so. I really want to speak to him again—an' not jest hear his voice inside my head."

"Now," declared Morey, "I have somethin' else fer ye. Somethin' I've been savin' fer jest the right moment."

Seeing their looks of puzzlement, he showed them his other hand, closed tight into a fist. Slowly, he opened his fingers, revealing what lay on his palm.

Shangri gasped, almost dropping the pastry. "It's . . . a ring."

"Right," her father agreed, watching her with delight. "Yer ma's wedding ring. I gave it to her after I'd earned enough to pay fer it . . . which took a fair while back in those days."

"That ring must have cost a lot of cinnamon buns," said Lorno. He, like Shangri, looked in awe at the beautiful copper ring. While streaks of green tarnished its edges, most of the ring still gleamed, shining as if it was lit from within.

Shangri gave the pastry to Lorno. Then she gently lifted the ring and slipped it onto her finger. It fit perfectly. Tears welled in her eyes, and she wrapped her arms around her father's neck.

"Thank ye so much, Papa." She sobbed quietly as she held him. "I'm the luckiest girl alive to have such a pa."

"An' I'm the luckiest pa," he answered, "to have such a girl."

Pulling slightly away so they could look at each other face to face, he corrected himself. "Yer not a girl, though. Not anymore. Yer a woman . . . a wonderful woman."

Wiping a tear off her cheek, she replied, "Yes . . . with a beautiful wedding ring."

Morey smiled at her. "Another kind o' magic circle."

CHAPTER 10

Banana Bread

Early the next morning, Atlanta sat at the small pinewood table in her kitchen. The first light of day sent shafts through the acacia and spruce trees surrounding her house, shafts that fell through the open kitchen window, brightening the whole room. Just outside the window, the day's first birdsong drifted in from a pair of curlews perched on a branch.

Atlanta took a sip of fresh mint tea from her favorite mug, carved from a burl by her friend Honya, a chimpanzee who was the most skilled woodcarver in the Great Forest. Reaching for the bowl of wildflower honey beside her, Atlanta spooned some into her mug and took another sip. Something about the combination of mint and honey always gave her a serene feeling of well-being.

As she drank her tea, Quiggley the faery

worked patiently to weave a few lilac vines into a hole in the shoulder of Atlanta's gown. The faery hovered in the air above the hole, his luminous blue wings whirring softly, as he inspected his progress. After one more tightening of a vine, he landed on her shoulder. Tilting his tiny cotton hat at a jaunty angle, he nodded with pride, then sent Atlanta a wave of satisfaction.

"Oh, thank you, little friend." Atlanta set down her mug and felt the newly repaired gown. "Beautiful work."

Quiggley crossed his arms and peered at her, as if to say, *Well, of course. What else?*

She grinned at him, well aware that clothing repair was the very least of his skills. Ever since she'd nursed him back to health after Grukarr had destroyed an entire faery colony that included Quiggley's family, the little fellow had proved himself to be her loyal friend and companion. As well as something more. As a rare lone faery, a quiggleypottle, he brought good luck that had on occasion saved Atlanta from harm—or death.

Suddenly the stove popped open. A loaf of fresh-baked banana bread, steaming hot, shot out and skidded across the table. It stopped right in front of Atlanta, filling her nostrils with the aroma of sweet, buttery bananas. At the same time, a bowl of butter and a knife flew out of the cupboard, landing right beside the loaf.

"Why, Etheria. What a wonderful surprise!" Atlanta winked at Quiggley, for both of them knew how the house dearly loved a compliment.

All the candles in the kitchen flared brighter. The window shutters clacked in approval. And the floorboards under Atlanta's chair shivered with delight.

Atlanta sliced a piece of banana bread, inhaling more of the wonderful smell. Breaking off a small chunk, she put it on her shoulder next to the faery, who released another wave of gratitude and started munching. Meanwhile, Atlanta spread butter on the rest and took a big bite.

Savoring the banana bread's sweet flavor in her mouth, she gazed around Etheria, the sentient house that had been her home for many years. She remembered vividly the moment she'd found the acorn that had grown to enormous size after it had been dropped by a squirrel near the Starstone. The crystal's power had magnified not only the acorn's size, but also its magic. After some diligent carpentry by Atlanta's friends the beavers and woodpeckers, and some help from a team of centaurs who hauled it to this spot, Atlanta had gladly moved in.

Right from the start, the acorn house had shown supreme devotion to Atlanta's comfort—as well as a rather quirky personality. If Atlanta had any visitors who might make a mess or leave muddy prints on the floor, Etheria would sprout thorns on her outside walls, slam the windows shut, and barricade the door. Porcupines (who often left quills behind) and centaurs (who often left something very smelly behind) were Etheria's least favorite visitors. Anytime Atlanta tried to coax Etheria to be more welcoming, the whole house closed up tight all its windows and cabinet doors, simply refusing to listen.

At this moment, however, Etheria was at her best, providing tea and breakfast. Atlanta took another bite of the warm banana bread.

"Nothing for me?" grumbled a plump squirrel from inside the cupboard's top drawer. The squirrel poked his furry brown head above the rim. Studying Atlanta with beady black eyes, he complained, "That's typical."

Atlanta shook her head, tossing her brown curls. "If you want some banana bread, Grumps, you'll have to ask nicely."

The squirrel glared at her. Then, pointing his bushy tail toward the faery on her shoulder, he complained, "You didn't make Babywings over there ask you nicely."

Quiggley frowned, sending a wave of indignation around the room. He set down his crumb of bread and raised both his tiny fists, ready to teach the surly squirrel a lesson.

"Hold on, little friend." Atlanta glanced over at Quiggley. "Let's just ignore him until he shows some better manners."

As both of them went back to eating, Grumps dived back down into the drawer. After a few seconds, the tip of his tail lifted out and knocked against the wood. "All right," came the muffled voice from inside the drawer. "May I *please* have some bread?"

"Yes," replied Atlanta. She sliced another piece and tossed it into the drawer. "Enjoy it."

No more words came from the squirrel . . . though there was the unmistakable sound of small teeth nibbling.

Casting her gaze again around her house, Atlanta felt grateful for the Starstone. Not only had its great powers made this home possible, those very powers had magnified every bit of magic in the forest. The dancing mist maidens who rose from streams, the singing fruits that hung from boughs, the birds whose every feather changed colors with those birds' moods, the many-tongued lizards who spoke several languages fluently, and countless other creatures—all of them owed their extraordinary gifts to the Starstone.

I'm so glad it's safely hidden on Moss Island, she reflected. *And I'm even gladder that Promi rescued it from all those dangers.*

She swallowed some more mint tea, recalling her amazing dream visit with Promi. He'd been so vividly present, so truly *with* her as they walked together and spoke earnestly, she had no doubt at all that it was real. While a whole week had passed since the dream, she could still hear Promi's voice, still feel his touch, still see the loving gleam in his eyes.

Sadly, he hadn't been able to tell her the most important thing he'd wanted to say. Etheria had woken her up just at that instant—jealous, no doubt, that Promi had come in her sleep. Yet . . . she had some idea of what he'd been hoping to tell her. Just the thought of that made her grin.

Let's hope, she told herself with another sip of tea, *he has another chance soon. Before too much more time goes by.*

A troubling fact about the spirit realm, she and Promi had discovered, was that time there moved far more slowly than on the world of mortals. So the week since his dream visit might have been only a day—or less—to Promi. And the gap between the two worlds' times could accelerate dramatically. While Promi and Atlanta had originally met when they were the same age, she was now already five years older. That age difference didn't seem to matter at all in their dream visit. But if a lot more years passed before they could truly be together . . . that could be a serious problem.

Her thoughts turned to more pressing problems right here on Atlantis. Although the vast mining operation where she'd met Shangri had been abandoned for the past week, Atlanta had no doubt that Reocoles would try to revive it. And probably expand it. Soon more soldiers and workers, plus more of those monstrous machines, would be tearing off soil and ripping down trees.

Sensing her change of mood, Etheria dimmed the candles in the kitchen. Quiggley, too, sensed the change. He leaped into the air and hovered in front of Atlanta's face. Though she felt a rush of compassion from the faery, it didn't help.

"What happens," she asked, "if those mining people move deeper into the forest? What if they put everything here at risk—including the Starstone?"

Wings humming, Quiggley frowned. He released a new feeling, one Atlanta recognized immediately.

Fear.

She set down her mug on the table. "Come on," she declared. "We're going to take a walk."

All the shelves in the kitchen sagged and the floorboards creaked as Etheria sighed in disappointment. But Atlanta merely patted the top of the table gently and then stood. As the faery landed on the collar of her gown of woven vines, she stepped over to the door.

Seeing Quiggley's quizzical expression, she said, "We're going to the Indragrass Meadows. To find the one person who might know what's going to happen. And what we can do about it."

CHAPTER 11

Endless Magic with You Goes

Several hours later, having walked through the western reaches of the Great Forest, Atlanta caught the distinct aroma of lemongrass. Even through the thick mesh of branches ahead, she saw a new openness beyond. Before long she stepped out of the trees and faced the wide, rolling fields of the Indragrass Meadows.

Stooping to pluck a sprig of lemongrass, she handed it to the faery perched on her collar. "Here you go, little friend."

He sent her a wave of gratitude, then started happily chewing on the sprig.

"Now," she announced, "we have to find Gryffion." Quiggley gave a vigorous nod, almost dislodging his tiny cotton hat.

Gryffion, eldest and wisest of the unicorns,

had spoken with Atlanta whenever she traveled to the Meadows. He'd even come once to call on her a few years ago, arriving unexpectedly at her home. The old unicorn had knocked politely on the door with his prominent horn so that Etheria would allow him to enter. It was on that visit that he'd shared some deeply disturbing news.

A new unicorn had just been born, the first new arrival in over a thousand years. Normally, that would have been cause for great celebration. But in reading the placenta for signs of the future, the unicorns had found a startling prophecy—that the isle of Atlantis would soon be lost forever.

Recalling Gryffion's words, Atlanta furrowed her brow. The unicorn had even spoken the same phrase that Haldor the centaur had used in his most gloomy prophecy—*a terrible day and night of destruction.*

From his perch on her collar, Quiggley fluttered his wings, gently brushing the skin of her neck. She felt a wave of compassion . . . along with an undercurrent of distress.

"Thanks," she said to the faery. Then she added her favorite words to say to a friend: "I bless your eternal qualities."

The hint of a smile appeared on his tiny face.

Topping a grassy hill, Atlanta faced the island's western shores. Thick fog from the sea completely shrouded the landscape ahead, hiding it from view. But she knew that beyond the fog lay the strange place called Mystery Bay. Home to creatures as varied as shape-shifting crocodiles, who might appear as harmless insects before suddenly attacking, and mighty dragons who decorated their caves with precious jewels, as well as their most cherished books, Mystery Bay held both dangers and allures.

Someday, Atlanta promised herself, *I'll go exploring there.*

A whir of wings by her neck reminded her of her passenger, and she added, *But not without you, little friend.*

The faery's antennae vibrated, sending her a rush of satisfaction.

The wind shifted, coming from the west, scattering some of the sea fog. Just then, a new sound reached the companions—a deep, powerful roar. Atlanta stiffened. Could that be an approaching dragon? She glanced around, desperately searching for someplace to hide. But the wide, treeless meadows offered no cover at all.

The roar continued, never pausing, pouring out of the fog as a sustained din. All at once, Atlanta laughed, shaking her head at her own foolishness. For she'd finally realized what the source of the roar really was.

"A waterfall!" she exclaimed. On her collar, Quiggley nodded.

Sure enough, sufficient fog had now parted to reveal a crashing cascade that flowed over a steep wall of polished rock. Curls of mist rose from the falls, mixing with the shredding fog; water sparkled in the growing light. All the while, the relentless roar of water continued, booming across the meadowlands.

Deciding to take a closer look, Atlanta strode toward the cascade. On her bare feet, she felt the growing wetness of the grass, soaked from the waterfall's spray and rising mist. With every breath, she tasted increased moisture in the air. Before long, a drop of water ran down the full length of her nose.

Suddenly she stopped. Staring at the waterfall, she stood frozen in surprise. The water wasn't falling at all! Rather, it was *rising*—flowing upward over the polished rock.

"Well," she said in astonishment. "This isn't a waterfall . . . but a *waterrise*." Continuing to peer at the upward-flowing river, she added, "Yet another mystery of Mystery Bay."

"Of which there are many," declared a deep baritone voice behind her.

Atlanta whirled around to see Gryffion, elegant as ever, standing in the grass. The unicorn's horn shimmered with a subtle radiance of its own, while his silver coat gleamed with water droplets. Even his mane, white with centuries of age, seemed to shine.

"To what," he asked politely, "do I owe this pleasure? It's been some time since we unicorns were visited by you and your quiggleypottle."

Atlanta bowed her head in respect. On her gown's collar, Quiggley clapped his antennae together.

"We need your advice," she explained. "People from the City—"

"I know all about that," interrupted Gryffion. Angrily, he stamped a silver hoof on the grass. "Word travels fast on this island. So I've heard much about the terrible deeds of some . . . and the heroic deeds of others. Including the two of you."

"Then you also know," she pressed, "that they are likely to come back. With more soldiers and bigger machines. I'm worried that this time, even with the help of the faeries and other forest creatures, we won't be able to stop them."

The elder unicorn shook his white mane. "Come with me, dear one. There is something you should see."

Gryffion turned and started to trot across the grass. His head bobbed with the cadence of his hooves, while the glow from his horn sent rays of light through the misty air. Running alongside him, Atlanta couldn't help but notice how lightly he stepped, like a breeze moving over a cloud.

As they came to a dark outcrop of rock, Gryffion slowed and then stopped. Without a word, he pointed his horn toward the other side of the outcrop. She stepped in that direction, wondering what he wanted her to see.

Behind the rock, a small stream coursed through meadow greenery. The water bubbled and swirled through its channel, constantly splashing the purple and red stones scattered along its path. And there, on the far bank, a playful young creature cavorted in the grass.

Atlanta caught her breath. *The young unicorn.*

Well aware that young unicorns stayed hidden for several decades until their magic had fully developed, Atlanta knew how unusual it was to see this particular animal. Enchanted, she watched intently. The unicorn's silver hooves flashed in the light as she pranced along the stream. Then she paused and bent her horn lower until it touched the ground. The horn's tip flashed. At that instant, a bright gold flower burst out of the soil, its petals shining like miniature suns.

Atlanta turned to the elder unicorn by her side and whispered, "She is a miracle."

"Indeed she is," Gryffion agreed. "Her name is Myala. In the unicorn Oldspeak, it means *the future*."

For another moment, they watched the young unicorn. Playfully, she created more colorful flowers—blues and greens, purples and browns, yellows and reds. Soon it looked as if someone had crushed a rainbow and sprinkled all the radiant pieces along the stream.

"Myala's name truly fits," said Gryffion. "For she is the future in every sense. Not only will she outlive all the rest of us, but whether or not she finds a mate, she will someday bring a new unicorn into the world."

Atlanta raised an eyebrow. "You mean . . . ?"

"Yes, that's right. A female unicorn has the power to reproduce by herself. So if—magic forbid—she were the only unicorn left in the world, she could still give birth."

From deep in his throat came a rich chuckle. "Because of that, my devoted mate never misses a chance to remind me that despite all my magic, she has more."

"Rightly so," said Atlanta with a grin.

She turned back to the young unicorn. Myala sensed this, somehow, and faced Atlanta. For a timeless moment, their gazes met—Atlanta's eyes of blue-green and Myala's of rich lavender.

You are beautiful, Myala, thought Atlanta.

So are you, the magical creature replied with a thought of her own.

After a few seconds more, Myala returned to making new flowers by the water.

Atlanta thought about the young unicorn's name. Was it a burden for her to have the weight of the future on her graceful shoulders?

Abruptly, Atlanta's expression darkened. Still watching the young unicorn, she said glumly, "Myala's magic can only survive if *she* survives."

Gryffion cocked his head, clearly asking her to continue.

Atlanta sighed. "If the forest is destroyed, then everything on this island is threatened. Nowhere is safe." Vehemently, she added, "We have to protect Atlantis from those greedy people!"

The old unicorn's voice dropped even lower than usual. "They are not the only threat."

She eyed him quizzically. "Meaning?"

"I sense, somehow, that Atlantis faces new dangers from the spirit realm. We may once again be attacked by those shadow-beings, the mistwraiths—and others."

"No!" exclaimed Atlanta, loud enough that the young unicorn instantly froze, ready to flee. But Gryffion quickly sent her a thought that calmed her. She went back to exploring the stream, though she didn't create any more flowers.

"I'm afraid so, Atlanta. For the past few days, which could be just hours in the spirit realm, I've sensed growing troubles there."

"That means," she said under her breath, "Promi is also in danger."

"*Everyone* is in danger."

An immense weight suddenly seemed to press down on Atlanta's body and mind, making it harder to breathe. Along with the weight came an overwhelming feeling worse than fright or concern, a feeling she hadn't known since her parents had vanished when she was just a small child.

Powerless, she thought. *I'm totally powerless. I can't help the forest. Or Promi. Or myself.*

The weight grew heavier. Not even the rush of compassion from Quiggley made her feel any better.

Something touched her forearm. The tip of Gryffion's horn pressed gently against her. At the same time, the horn began to glow brighter, strengthening in radiance.

Slowly, very slowly, that very radiance seeped into Atlanta. The weight pushing down on her eased a little, then eased some more. At last, she drew a deep breath.

She shook herself, feeling her old strength again. Gratefully, she eyed Gryffion.

"Do you remember," the unicorn asked softly, "what advice I gave you that time we visited in the forest? When you felt the darkness deepening all around?"

The young woman nodded. "You said . . . *be a candle.*"

"That's right, dear one. Bring whatever light you can into the darkness."

Atlanta straightened herself. "I will try."

He studied her with compassion. "That's all we mortals can do."

Then, with a shake of his mane, he said, "Now I have a gift for you. Nothing physical, mind you, since physical things have only limited power. Why, even the Starstone's greatness comes not from the crystal but from the magic it holds."

"What is it?"

The unicorn's eyes gleamed. "A blessing. The oldest and most cherished blessing of the unicorns, one that is spoken only in times of great peril."

Gryffion lifted his luminous horn skyward. Seeing this, the young unicorn turned toward him, ears aquiver. Then, in his richly toned voice, he spoke:

> *Endless magic with you goes*
> *Bearing light where darkness grows.*
> *Higher even than the star*
> *Lighting planets from afar;*
> *Deeper even than the sea*
> *Where the whalesongs rise and fall*
> *Heeding ancient oceans' call—*
> *Reaches magic, pure and free.*
> *Endless magic with you goes*
> *Bringing triumph over foes.*
> *Wider even than the world*
> *Bearing marvels brightly pearled;*
> *Slimmer even than the moon*
> *Slice of light beyond the clouds*
> *Rising clear above the shrouds—*
> *Stretches magic, timeless boon.*
> *Endless magic with you goes*
> *Seeking rest beyond all woes.*
> *Nearer even than the soul*
> *Giving meaning to the goal;*
> *Farther even than the years*
> *Counted long before your birth*
> *Times of sorrow, mystery, mirth—*
> *Touches magic, have no fears.*
> *All this magic goes with you*
> *Guiding onward ever true.*
> *Breathe compassion, sing of hope*
> *Freely may you leap and lope.*

Give you gratitude and peace,
Strength to climb the mountain steep,
Courage when you laugh or weep—
Magic's blessings never cease.

After a moment of silence, Atlanta quietly repeated, "Magic's blessings never cease."

"Yes," answered the old unicorn. Lifting a forehoof from the grass, he reached toward her. She took the silver hoof in her hand, holding it tight.

Together, they said, "I bless your eternal qualities."

CHAPTER 12

A Dark Passage

*N*arkazan flew alone, his rail-thin body weaving in and out of the clouds. Traveling solo, he knew well, could be dangerous if the allies of Sammelvar and Escholia ever caught him. But the greater danger was being seen by one of their spies, so flying alone was preferable because it would draw less attention.

Darting behind a tufted blue cloud, the warlord spirit grumbled to himself, "The time will come when I won't need to hide from *any-one*. Certainly not that scoundrel Sammelvar or his army of wind lions!"

Spotting a family of winged serpents, whose scales radiated the green of emeralds and the blue of sapphires, he veered inside the cloud. For he knew that they, like so many others in the spirit realm, remained loyal to Sammelvar and Escholia. Cold, wet air flowed over him, drenching his creamy satin robe. Whenever his battered earring clinked against one of his tusks, a shower of droplets sprayed his face.

Finally, sensing the serpents had passed, he shot out of the cloud. Angrily, he shook himself to dry off. With a wrathful growl he continued toward his destination.

"I have waited much time to return," he snarled. "Too much time."

Narkazan dropped into a dark tunnel amidst the clouds, a narrow passage that he knew well. Though many shadows filled the tunnel—some of them darkened portals to other worlds, some of them travelers who preferred to stay hidden—he didn't need any light to find his way. This route would bring him right to the place where he'd long wanted to return.

"That is where I'll make my new battle plans," he growled. The tunnel's winds howled around him, swallowing his words. "And that is where, one day soon, I shall rule everything in the spirit and mortal realms."

Snaking through the dark passage, he tapped one of his tusks thoughtfully. "No one will expect me to go back there." He chortled, adding, "Just as no one will expect me to attack in the way I will."

Noticing a mass of dark beings flying toward him, Narkazan suddenly wondered if they could be some of his own mistwraiths. He swung to one side to watch as they came closer—then realized that they were not his shadowy troops. Instead, this was a flock of nightwings, airy black beasts who loved to soar freely in the darkness.

As the birds flew past, their wispy feathers making a deep *whooooosh* with every wingbeat, he thought about the command he'd given to his mistwraiths. "They'd better find Promi, that miserable scum of the Prophecy!" He scowled. "I have some important matters to discuss with him."

Clenching both fists, he flew faster. "And they'd also better find my precious Starstone. The sooner the better! We have much work to do, that crystal and I."

He chortled again. "Just as the mortal monster of that pool has much work to do. Pleasant, enjoyable work."

Veering into a side tunnel, Narkazan pushed through a heavy wall of mist. Suddenly, he burst into the light. There, right before him, was his destination.

"Arcna Ruel," he said with pride. Quickly, to avoid being seen by any foes, he hid behind a billowing cloud that continually belched dark vapors from its top like a volcano made of mist. Safely hidden, Narkazan hovered, admiring the sight of his imposing cloud castle.

Darker than a thundercloud and far more terrible, Arcna Ruel had been built long ago by his servants. Made from supercondensed vaporstone, it was strong enough to withstand any attack, yet light enough to float freely. Six gigantic turrets towered over the battlements, surrounding an enormous dome that housed the Great Hall, a regal space whose inner walls gleamed pure white. This castle had once housed the Starstone—and, if the warlord had his way, would soon again.

Pausing, Narkazan peered closely at the castle before going any nearer. It seemed more still than death, an utterly abandoned structure far from the populous parts of the realm. No signs anywhere of enemy spies. Finally ready to enter, he left the billowing cloud and flew toward Arcna Ruel.

As he flew closer, he made some mental notes about how to fortify the structure militarily. Starting with the fact that currently no warriors patrolled the encircling wall.

That will soon change, he silently vowed. *As will everything else in this realm.*

His fists clenched so hard they turned deathly white. *For it is time, at last, to begin my War of Glory.*

Landing in an interior courtyard, Narkazan paused again to check his surroundings. All seemed in order; he sensed no signs of any intruders—or any life at all. Only himself, the once-great leader who would rise again, crushing all his enemies and conquering everything in the spirit and mortal realms.

Tapping one of his tusks thoughtfully, he promised himself, *The next time I enter this place, it will be as the greatest, most-powerful warrior-king of all time.*

He strode across the courtyard, holding his head high. When he reached the massive doors to the Great Hall, he threw them open. They slammed against the inner walls with a loud crash, sending reverberations around the dome overhead.

Narkazan stood there, alone, listening to the dome's vibrations. He remembered vividly how crowded this hall had been in the days before he'd been overthrown by that menace Promi. Back then it had teemed with hundreds of warriors, training and arming themselves all through the day and night. Now, however, the hall was an empty shell, devoid of any activity.

Drawing a full breath, he bellowed, "I have returned!"

His voice echoed around the dome, fading with each passing second. After a moment, the hall fell again into complete silence.

Then . . . he heard a sound. A faint crackling, from somewhere behind the walls, grew steadily louder. Suddenly, dozens of mist-wraiths emerged from the cracks in the vaporstone walls and floor. Like a gathering storm, the shadowy beings appeared in the center of the Great Hall, crackling vengefully as they sprayed black sparks.

At the same time, other immortal warriors arrived. Some, like the fierce red-winged dragon and the band of flying insects with enormous tongues, came by the air. Others came by the floor, emerging from secret passageways and hidden rooms, crawling and slithering and marching in unison. Many of them bore weaponry, including a troop of archers with powerful bows and arrows that glistened darkly. And even more of them carried their weapons on their bodies—deadly claws, blade-sharp teeth, and clubbed tails.

As he watched the assembling army, Narkazan showed no hint of emotion. He just scowled at the scene, his fiery eyes observing everything. At last, the final warrior arrived—a liquid beast that bubbled up through a crack in the floor, shrieking angrily.

Narkazan raised a bony hand. All the warriors instantly fell silent.

For several seconds, their commander studied them quietly. Then he spoke, his raspy voice filling the hall.

"Our long-awaited time has arrived," he declared. "Are you ready to fight?"

A deafening roar of cheers, hisses, snarls, and shrieks erupted. Narkazan listened, still betraying no emotion. Again he raised his hand, and again the soldiers fell silent.

"Good," their leader declared. "All of you are the leaders of your groups. By now, you know your instructions. And you also know the three basic rules of my army: No mercy. No mistakes. No rest until we have triumphed completely over all our foes."

Another loud roar burst from the soldiers, rattling the dome. A slab of vaporstone broke off from the ceiling and crashed to the floor, exploding into shards.

Narkazan gave a sharp nod. Instantly, the warriors formed themselves into precise units. The insects with twisting tongues hovered close together, the archers formed crisp lines, and the liquid beast shrank down into a mound of bubbling froth.

Surveying his soldiers, the warlord rasped, "First, we shall attack at the place our enemies least expect. Ready the flashbolt cannon!"

A giant warrior with amber skin and four burly arms nodded obediently. "As you command, master," he boomed.

"The rest of you," Narkazan continued, "go straight to your attack positions. Let no one see you travel there. Then wait in secret until the battle comes to you—which, I promise, it will."

Tails slammed the floor, beaks snapped shut, and many hands saluted.

"Above all," the warlord declared, "remember that you have been granted the honor of serving in what will always be called the great War of Glory."

At last, Narkazan's face showed a hint of emotion, as his upper lip curled into something like a malicious grin. "For glory will surely be mine."

CHAPTER 13

The Crystal Dove

The crystal dove, one of the rarest creatures on the isle of Atlantis, glided over the northern reaches of the Great Forest. Sailing high above the glades where spirals of mist rose along with the songs and chatter of countless birds and other creatures, she spread her crystalline wings to the widest. An updraft above a waterfall carried her still higher, as the sun rose above the horizon to greet the day.

The dove's wings, made of living glass, were completely transparent—except for their constant explosions of brilliant colors. For every single feather on those wings acted as an airborne prism whose facets radiated sparks and ribbons of greens, purples, yellows, blues, and reds that shifted and merged endlessly. No creature in this forest was more shocking, more beautiful, or more unforgettable than the crystal dove.

Gliding northward, she suddenly flapped her glass wings in surprise. Below her, the forest abruptly ended! Instead of the woodland home she knew so well, a new landscape had been brutally carved—a landscape that bore no resemblance to its origins.

Gone were the trees, rivers, and animal dens that had long filled the area. In their place sprawled Reocoles's industrial site, a vast complex of open pit mines, ditches, piles of tailings, buildings, and machines that looked like giant jaws on wheels. Though the machines sat quiet for now, it wasn't hard to imagine them coming to life with a deafening roar, pouring black smoke as they gouged at the land.

In fact, at that very moment, a large group of people was leaving the City of Great Powers to walk to the mines. While the complex had been shut down for several days since the "troubles," as Reocoles called the brief rebellion, this morning marked the resumption of work. Motivated by the unusually large amounts of money Reocoles was offering (and the lack of other work in the City), many men and women signed on. More than a hundred laborers and at least twenty uniformed soldiers marched across one of the bridges over the roaring river. Leading them, riding in a coal-fired wagon, was Reocoles's foreman—a thin man whose distinguishing qualities were his long, curly mustache and his unending sneer.

Tugging at one end of his mustache, Karpathos called to the group behind him, "Hurry now, you vermin! That extra pay I offered you won't be around if you take all day to get there."

Although some people heeded the command and walked faster, most of the group continued to shuffle slowly across the bridge. Maybe they couldn't hear Karpathos's cry because of the din of the river. But they moved more like prisoners under duress than people starting a new job.

Lagging behind the group, far enough away that they weren't likely to be noticed, came three more people. Shangri led the way. With a grim expression and her red hair secured by a kerchief, she occasionally glanced at the copper ring that now adorned her finger. Right behind her walked Lorno, a frown on his face and a bulge in his tunic from all the pastries that Morey had stuffed into his pocket. (Morey himself had wanted to join them, but Shangri pleaded with him to stay at the bakery so that Reocoles wouldn't suspect anything.) Last of all sauntered Graybeard, his collection of knives jiggling inside his ragged old coat. Of the three, he was the only one who seemed to be enjoying the journey.

Shangri and her companions hadn't planned to leave at the same time as the work crew. In fact, they had simply left at dawn to head into the forest, guided by the magical compass from Atlanta. But when they reached the bridge, they realized that Reocoles, too, had big plans for that day. By then, the people going to the mines had already started over the bridge. Shangri knew that it would take more time to circle around to a different bridge than to wait for the laborers to cross.

Never someone with much patience, she fumed to herself, *The sun will be overhead by the time we're across this bleedin' bridge!*

Lorno, sensing her distress, stepped up to her and took her hand. Though he said no words, the touch of his hand helped Shangri feel calmer. Yet she knew, as he did, that this would be a long and dangerous day.

Meanwhile, at the mining complex, the crystal dove circled, trying to make sense of the scene below. Then something even stranger than all the desolation caught her attention. At the center of the site sat a large pool unlike any lake she'd ever seen. Rather than shining clear blue, with reflections of the pink and peach rays of the sunrise, this lake was dark yellow. No reflections at all showed on its surface; no plants of any kind grew on its shores.

With a brilliant flash of colors from her glass wings, the bird swooped lower. Seeing no tree branches nearby to perch on, she settled on the roof of one of the abandoned machines. Curious to understand this strange sight, she moved to the edge nearest to the pool.

Leaning closer to the yellow liquid, she instantly noticed the smell. Rancid, like something very rotten, the smell struck her like a foul wind. She fluttered her prismatic wings, backing away.

Yet her curiosity proved stronger than her revulsion. Cautiously, she moved back to the edge. Steeling herself to the smell, she peered down at the liquid.

Bubbles! She clacked her crystalline beak in surprise to see bubbles rising from the center of the pool. Like a slowly boiling broth, the liquid churned as the bubbles rose steadily to the surface.

Instinct told the dove that those bubbles weren't rising solely from whatever ingredients were mixing in the pool. No, something else lay in those depths, hidden from sight. Something alive.

Something breathing.

Stirring.

Waiting.

The dove couldn't have known that this pool held a beast spawned by the hatred of Narkazan. A beast that had struggled mightily to be born . . . and to satisfy its growing hunger. Several times, in the dark of night, it had reached part of its body above the surface—only to fall back into the putrid pool, still too weak to emerge.

Even so, the crystal dove realized that only something evil could be lurking down there. Panicked, she knew she must go!

She beat her glass wings, flashing rainbows as she lifted into the air. Feeling the safety of the sky, she flapped again, releasing a new burst of radiance. Like a living prism, she made the air shimmer with dazzling colors.

At that very instant, a long black tongue shot out of the pool. Before the dove could rise any higher, the tongue wrapped around her entire body. Squeezing in a death grip, the tongue shattered her feathers and bones and drew her down into the churning depths.

The pool fell still again. After a few seconds, even the ripples on the surface disappeared. No sign of the crystal dove—or the tongue that had ended her life—remained. As before, bubbles drifted lazily to the surface.

Suddenly, a gargantuan shape exploded from the pool. Yellow liquid rained down on the mining complex as the monster clambered ashore, dragging its immense body onto the rocks. Its skin shone the same putrid yellow color as the toxic pool, except for small dark lumps across its back that could have been festering sores. Awkward in this new environment, it rolled as much as it lurched on its stubby legs. Raising its bulbous head to the sky, it released a roar so loud that it shook the trees all around.

Lurching forward, the toadlike monster paused to gulp the air, eagerly swallowing something far more pleasant than the liquid of the pool. After several more gulps, it sniffed the air with its cavernous nostrils.

All at once it froze. Smelling a hint of what it most desired, what it hoped would satisfy its burning hunger, the monster spun around to face a certain direction. The direction of the City.

Its eyes—wells of utter darkness, deeper than any chasm and emptier than any void—peered into the distance. As if they could see beyond the mines, beyond the dirt road, beyond the gates to the settlement itself, they stared hungrily. For this beast needed food, enormous quantities of food, both to feed its mortal body . . . and also for another purpose known only to itself and Narkazan.

With a sudden lurch, the monster from the toxic pool set out to find the City. The people and buildings there. And the food it required.

Behind on the ground, it left a trail of putrid slime . . . as well as a few shards of shattered glass.

CHAPTER 14

Swallows

The monster's wrathful roar echoed across the denuded hills that lay between the industrial site and the City. Having recently crossed the bridge over the river, all the people in the work crew heard it—and all of them halted in their tracks. Anxiously, they looked at their neighbors. What could that bellowing cry be? What kind of beast could have made it?

Only Karpathos didn't stop. Chugging ahead on his coal-fired cart, he merely twisted both ends of his mustache. *Foolish vermin,* he cursed to himself. *Now they'll use that noise, whatever it was, as an excuse to go even slower.*

Before the monster's roar erupted, Shangri and her two companions had also crossed the bridge. But rather than follow the dirt road that led to the mines, they veered toward the deep forest. Just before they stepped into the trees, Shangri glanced again at her ring—then over at Lorno. He'd been watching her, and gave her an encouraging smile. Feeling a bit more confident, she took the magical compass out of her pocket.

"Open now," she commanded, resting her arm against her torso to hold it steady. Immediately, the crumpled leaf unfurled, flattening on the palm of her hand. Lorno and Graybeard looked on, watching intently.

"Show me the way," Shangri urged. Obediently, the piece of amber spun around and pointed due south—toward the heart of the Great Forest. That way, they would find Atlanta.

Just then the monster's roar shook the very ground where they stood. Although they were still close enough to the laborers and soldiers on the road that they could hear voices, they knew that the roar hadn't come from those people. What, then, had made such a terrible cry?

"I have the same ugly feelin'," said Shangri with a shudder, "that I had jest before seein' the mines. Somethin' bad is about to happen, fer certain."

Graybeard gently placed his hand on her shoulder. "Worry not, young one. That's probably nothing more than a natural sound from the forest."

Though his melodic voice had its usual soothing quality, this time Shangri's intuition was stronger. She shook her head so hard that tufts of red hair sprang out from under her kerchief. Looking straight at the thin man's face, she declared, "Whatever that sound be, it weren't natural."

"I agree," declared Lorno. "It sounded more like a beast of some kind. A very angry beast."

"Nonsense," said Graybeard soothingly. "In any case, we shouldn't let anything distract ourselves from our mission—to find that young woman of the woods! Atlanta, I believe you called her."

Shangri looked at him uncertainly. Despite his reassuring voice . . . something about his words didn't seem quite right. "That's her name, yes. But findin' her isn't our mission. Findin' her is jest the first step o' what's *really* our mission—stoppin' Reocoles from destroyin' this whole forest."

"Sure, sure, I agree," said Graybeard hurriedly. "That's really what I meant."

Shangri nodded, setting aside her doubts. Something about the man's voice made her, well, *want* to agree with him. Whatever he said.

"So," said Graybeard in a jaunty tone, "shall we enter the forest? The sooner we find Atlanta, the sooner we can get on with our plans."

"All right," she said, carefully returning the compass to her pocket. Facing Lorno, she asked, "Are ye ready?"

"Absolutely," he declared. "Nothing can delay us now, short of—"

Another terrible roar rocked them, scaring a flock of swallows out of the trees at the forest edge. The birds rose skyward, chattering noisily. At the same time, over among the laborers, several people screamed in fright.

Shangri caught Lorno's eye. Both of them knew that this time, the roar had come from somewhere closer. Much closer.

Suddenly, at the far end of the road leading to the mines, a huge, hulking form appeared. Dark yellow, with only bottomless wells for eyes, it leaped toward the laborers like a monstrous toad. From its gigantic, tooth-studded mouth drooled rivers of yellow slime. And as it approached, that mouth opened wider.

"Holy Hephaestus!" shrieked Karpathos, turning his vehicle so sharply that it careened into a ditch, hurling him onto the ground.

Just as the foreman crawled away from the wreckage and started to stand, a great black appendage slammed down onto the wagon.

The monster's tongue! Boards splintered, wheels crumpled, and lumps of coal flew into the air.

Astonished, Karpathos stared as the tongue wrapped itself around the iron casing of the vehicle's motor. With unearthly power, the tongue squeezed, crunching the metal down into a smaller heap. Then, lightning quick, the tongue withdrew—carrying the metal right into the monster's mouth.

Laborers and soldiers scattered. Screaming with terror, they ran away from the road or back toward the City, anywhere to get away from this horrid beast. Cries of panic and desperation filled the air.

None of those people ran fast enough, though, to escape the tongue. Like a cracking whip, the tongue slashed through the air, grabbing men and women for this long-awaited feast. One man, caught by the leg, dug his bloody fingers into the dirt as he was dragged into the beast's gaping mouth. A rumbling gulp—and his wailing cries suddenly ended.

With every swallow, the monster grew a bit bigger. Still drooling slime, it lurched and waddled down the road, picking off as many people as possible. Every time it nabbed a victim, that person's heartrending screams ended with the same sickening gulp.

Shangri and her companions, standing far off the road by the forest edge, watched with horror. The massacre continued, swallow after swallow, as did the wailing screams. And there was nothing they could do but witness it all.

"No!" wailed Shangri. "We've got to do somethin'!"

"What?" asked Lorno, grabbing her by the arm. Shaking from the ghastly scene, he said, "Go out there and you'll just get eaten yourself."

"He's right," Graybeard chimed in. Tapping his coat, he added, "My knives would be worthless against that monster."

"But we can't jest . . . ," said Shangri, choking back tears, "leave them all to die." Under her breath, she added, "This beast has somethin' to do with those mine pits, I'm certain."

"The best thing we can do," Graybeard said soothingly, "is to enter the forest now. Follow the compass. And find Atlanta."

Shangri released a sorrowful sigh. "All right. Let's get movin'."

As the monster roared again, louder than ever, the companions darted into the forest. They vanished among the trees without a trace, as if they'd been swallowed completely.

CHAPTER 15

Searching

hick greenery enveloped them.
Fallen branches, coated with
mosses and lichens, covered the
ground. Sturdy vines draped
down from the towering trees. Huge spider-
webs glistened in the shadows. All these obsta-
cles, as well as the uneven turf, made walking
treacherous.

Even so, they forged ahead. With Shangri
and her compass in the lead, the trio crashed
their way deeper into the forest. But the farther
they went, tripping and struggling through all
the growth, the thicker the forest became.

Making matters worse, they saw no signs of
any trails for people. Only a narrow path to a
fox's den, a row of bright pebbles arranged by
a bowerbird to attract a mate to his nest, and a
line through moist moss left by a passing snake.

Shangri clambered over a toppled tree trunk,

only to catch her apron on one of its broken branches. Angrily, she yanked the apron—tearing a big hole in it.

"Plagues in me puddin'!" she cursed. "This is goin' to be harder than we thought."

"Much harder," agreed Graybeard, trying to pull his coat out of the clutches of a thorn bush.

As if in agreement, a great horned owl hooted soulfully from the branches of an ancient yew tree that arched overhead.

Lorno wiped a strand of spider's web off his face. "How are we supposed to get help from Atlanta if we can't even reach her?"

"An' how," demanded Shangri, "are we goin' to stop that monster from the mines before it gulps down everythin' on this island?"

Lorno put his hand on her shoulder. "I'll tell you how. By not giving up."

Shangri looked at him doubtfully.

"If we give up," the young bard said, "then we're lost for sure. But if we keep going, even as tough as this is . . ."

"Then at least," finished Shangri, "we have a chance." She sucked in her breath and watched him, her eyes a tiny bit brighter. "I knew I married ye for some reason."

Peering at her compass again, she watched the amber point the way deeper into the forest. "Let's be goin', then."

"Whatever you say," said Lorno with a squeeze of her shoulder.

They set off, followed by Graybeard, who had only just extracted his coat from the thorns. Grimly, he patted the cloth over his knives, feeling their hard metal blades underneath. *Patience,* he told himself. *Your time will come.*

After another few hours of struggles—including when Lorno slipped and plunged into a marshy pool, scattering frogs and dragonflies everywhere—they reached the edge of a small knoll. Seeing the sunlight dancing on the ferns and grasses at the top, Shangri led them up there. For the first time that whole morning, they could feel warm rays of sunshine on their faces, as well as a breath of fragrant wind.

Lifting her face to the sky, Shangri closed her eyes to soak in the new sensations. "I'm wishin' we could find her right here," she said wistfully.

"We won't," answered Lorno. "But we just might find her over there."

She turned to see where he was pointing. Beyond the flowering bushes at the base of the knoll ran a flowing line of smooth grass that disappeared into the trees. A trail.

Catching her breath, Shangri checked the compass. It pointed in the same direction as the trail!

Swiftly, they hurried down the knoll. Setting foot on the trail, their moods lifted immediately. Despite her torn apron and the scratches on her arms, Shangri felt a renewed surge of strength.

As she and Lorno started down the grassy path, Graybeard watched them with the unblinking eyes of a predator. *Lead on,* he silently urged them. *I have important work to do.*

CHAPTER 16

Something to Say

Worries crowded Promi's mind as he flew through the mists of the spirit realm on the way to Atlantis. Would Narkazan's mistwraiths get there before him? Would Atlanta's life already be in danger? Would they succeed in protecting the Starstone?

He banked a turn through a stream of golden clouds that flowed so fast it whipped up a wind that fluttered the cloth of his tunic and tousled his hair. Thinking about those worries, he rode the wind for as long as he could to gain speed. But nothing could help him fly fast enough.

Atlanta's in trouble, he told himself. *I'm sure of it.*

The skin on his chest prickled with heat as it always did when he felt anxious. The mark of the soaring bird above his heart seemed to burn, even as his pounding heart made the bird's wings vibrate under his tunic. Not since he'd faced a lone mistwraith in Narkazan's lair had his skin felt as hot as it did right now. It was much worse than any anxious heat he'd felt in his years as a thief on the streets of the City, when his riskiest exploits were stealing a smackberry pie from under the nose of the Divine Monk and relieving the evil priest Grukarr of his belt buckle (as well as his pants).

Breaking out of the stream of golden clouds, he plunged into a forest of misty trees that were swiftly evolving into tall, perpendicular worlds. Passing close to one of those worlds, he glimpsed a city of needle-thin spires.

Slicing through that place, he entered a new zone of swirling mist and constant cyclones that often knocked travelers off course. But he'd passed through those maelstroms before on his way to Earth, so he knew the risks well. Besides, that was the fastest route to finding Atlanta.

Sharp winds slammed into him. Yet even with gusts tearing at his body and screeching in his ears, he kept his bearings. Fighting against the winds that hit him from all sides, he surged ahead.

Suddenly he broke free of the cyclones, entering the upper atmosphere of one world he knew especially well. The world of Atlantis . . . and the person he most wanted to see. The person he cared for more than any other.

This time, he vowed, *I'll tell her. Whatever happens, I'm going to finish that sentence!*

Seconds later, he saw the misty outline of an island in the vast blue ocean. Approaching rapidly, he peered down at its craggy cliffs, mysterious vales, and lively rivers. There, in its center, he saw the swath of deep green that was the Great Forest. Atlanta's home.

Feeling a rush of pride, he recalled that frightful moment when he'd made an utterly impossible plea to all the sources of magic in the world—and a terrible sacrifice to go with it—that had somehow created Atlantis. *Not bad*, he thought, *for a rascally thief.*

Surprised, he noticed a patch of bare ground at the northern edge of the forest. *That's strange*, he thought. *Haven't seen that before.*

Drawing nearer, he saw the pits that scarred that spot and glimpsed what looked like a yellow lake. What could that be? All around the site, some sort of machinery sat unused. And several buildings dotted the area, though he saw no signs of people.

All at once, he realized what this place was. The industrial site built by the Greeks from that ship he'd saved! The place he'd heard about from Atlanta in their dream visit and from Shangri in her prayer.

Promi clenched his jaw, flying his fastest. *The Greek sailors may have done that . . . but I caused it.* He gnashed his teeth, wishing he hadn't called to the great goddess of the sea, O Washowoe-myra, to save those sailors from drowning. Yet how could he have known what troubles they would bring to the most magical place on Earth?

Plunging toward the forest, he steered toward the spot where he guessed he'd find Atlanta. Whether or not she already knew of the grave danger to the Starstone, she might have gone to that spot just to enjoy its magic—magic that radiated more powerfully than anywhere else in the forest, since the Starstone itself was hidden there. After all, he'd found her there many times before.

Moss Island.

Swiftly, he approached the deep green patch of land surrounded by streams that splashed incessantly. In its center grew a towering willow tree, majestic and delicate at the same time, its tresses draping over the moss like a living curtain. And there, sitting cross-legged on one of the willow's gnarled roots, was Atlanta.

Promi landed right in front of her, his bare feet sinking deep into the moss. Instantly, she jumped to her feet. The faery on her collar took flight, blue wings whirring, and settled on a willow branch, just as Atlanta darted over to Promi and embraced him.

But this was not, he sensed right away, one of her joyful, rollicking hugs. She buried her face into the nape of his neck, holding tight as someone drowning would hold onto anything that might float.

She lifted her face so they were nose to nose. "This isn't," she asked softly, "another dream visit, is it? Because . . . I'd really like to be with *you* just now. The real you."

Promi watched the lovely curl of her lips as she spoke, feeling her warm breath on his cheeks. He could feel, as well, the strong pulsing of her heart against his chest. He took a deep breath of the forest air, so sweet with resins and rich with the aromas of plants and trees.

"It's the real me."

She smiled, but her smile vanished as swiftly as a jaguar slips into the evening shadows. "Oh, Promi. Terrible things are happening! Worse even than what those people are doing with their mines is what I just learned from Gryffion, eldest of the unicorns. There's grave danger to—"

"The Starstone." He peered into the deep pools of her blue-green eyes. "From those phantoms of the spirit realm, the mistwraiths who serve Narkazan. He wants the crystal back. And this time, he'll stop at nothing to turn it into his ultimate weapon."

Atlanta gasped. "So it's true."

"Too true, I'm afraid." Instinctively, Promi glanced down at the magical dagger on his belt, noticing the icicle-like blade and the silver string that would wrap around his wrist whenever he threw it.

Following his glance, Atlanta remembered that he'd been given that dagger right here on Moss Island. It was a parting gift from the river god Bopaparrúplio, who had suddenly appeared out of the waters of the stream after the mist maidens' entrancing dance. Yet . . . as magical as that blade was, Atlanta—like Promi—knew it would be useless against an attack by mistwraiths.

Turning back to Promi, she asked, "What are we going to do?"

He swallowed, then said, "I don't know yet what we're going to do about the Starstone. But Atlanta . . . there's something else I have to do. Right now, before I lose my chance."

Another swallow, then he added, "Or my courage."

Loosening her embrace on him, she tilted her head. "Is it . . . something you've been wanting to say?"

"For a very long time." Studying her face, he said, "Though speaking of time, you don't seem that much older. To me, our dream visit was just a day ago. It hasn't been months or years for you, I hope?"

She almost grinned. "Just a week." Mischievously, she added, "But I'm still a few years older than you now. Which makes me *much* wiser."

"That's always been true," he said with a smirk. "Even when we were the same age."

Sitting above them on the willow branch, Quiggley nodded vigorously.

"So, Promi . . . what was it you wanted to say?"

"What I wanted to tell you in our dream. What I was just starting to say when you suddenly woke up."

She linked her arms around his waist. "Well, you can tell me now. This is your chance. But before you do, there's one little thing I want to say to *you*."

Before he could object, she kissed him on the lips. A long, tender kiss that made his eyes open wide in surprise.

Above them, Quiggley rolled his eyes. He shook his head, as if to say, *How do these people ever get anything done if it takes them so long to say what they want to say?*

As the kiss ended, Promi whispered in a slightly hoarse voice, "That wasn't a little thing."

"Maybe not," she answered brightly. "But it needed to be said. Now it's your turn."

Watching, Quiggley folded his arms. With one of his tiny red berry shoes, he tapped the branch impatiently.

"Well," Promi began, "what I, um . . . wanted to say, is . . ."

"Yes?"

"Something I haven't said before. Or really . . . haven't *wanted* to say before." He swam, for an imaginary moment, in those blue-green pools. "To anyone."

"Yes?" she repeated.

"Anyone at all."

Warmly, she said, "You can tell me, Promi."

He gazed at her. At last, he said, "Atlanta. You need to know this."

She waited expectantly.

He cleared his throat, then declared, "I really do—"

"Atlanta!" shouted another voice. "And Promi—you're here!"

Promi's mouth moved to say the final words of that sentence . . . but no sounds came. Both of them turned toward the new voice.

CHAPTER 17

The Visitors

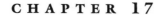

Atlanta and Promi whirled around to see someone running toward them through the forest. Even through the willow tree's curtain of leaves, they couldn't mistake who it was.

Shangri. Red-faced, she looked both tired and frightened as she sped through some waist-high ferns. Her kerchief dangled from the tangles of her hair, while burrs and broken twigs clung to her torn baker's apron. Scratches covered her arms. In her hand, she clutched Atlanta's compass.

Right behind her came Lorno, looking several years older than the last time Promi had seen him on the day the shipload of Greeks had arrived. And not far behind him came someone neither Promi nor Atlanta had seen before, a tall fellow with a gray beard. While the beard and his tattered coat made him seem unremarkable, even harmless, something about his dark, intelligent eyes told a different story.

Shangri splashed across the stream, spraying the moss that grew so thickly on the island. Breathless, she ran over to her friends and practically fell into their arms.

"Shangri," asked Atlanta, "what is it?"

"Catch your breath," added Promi. "Then tell us."

"No time . . . to catch me breath," she panted, standing upright. "We heard it . . . the roar! Then it came . . . so fierce. Right out o' the mines! Roarin' . . . an' chargin' straight at them. Devourin' all those poor people!"

"What?" demanded Atlanta. "What are you talking about?"

"The monster," declared Lorno, stepping out of the stream. "We saw it attack! Those people . . . they never had a chance."

"What monster?" asked Promi.

"What people?" pressed Atlanta.

Above them on the branch, Quiggley shuddered. Then the faery glided down to Atlanta, settling again on her collar.

"By the mines," explained Shangri, trying to regain her composure. "A monster, like a giant toad! Attackin' any person in its path."

"Or any*thing*," added Lorno. "Remember what it did to that wagon?"

"I'll never forget," said the older man, wading across to the island. As soon as he reached the mossy bank, he stamped his boots to dry them off. Then, shoving aside some of the willow's leafy branches, he peered at the others and lamented, "It was terrible. A slaughter."

Atlanta shot Promi a worried glance. "Where," she wondered aloud, "did this monster come from?"

"Narkazan?" guessed Promi.

"Maybe," Shangri answered. "But I jest can't shake the feelin' that it came from the mines themselves. It's like . . . all that greed made itself into a livin' nightmare."

Quiggley nodded his little head, releasing a wave of agreement so strong that everyone felt it.

Suddenly taking note of the faery, Shangri caught her breath. "Why, it's you! The brave little fellow who saved us when we was fightin' fer our lives."

The barest hint of a blush colored Quiggley's cheeks. He bowed in greeting.

Captivated, Shangri gave him a curtsy. Turning back to Atlanta, she blurted, "I was jest so worried an' scared . . . I forgot to say how glad I am to see ye again."

Atlanta reached out her hand and touched Shangri's arm. "And I'm glad to see you. Now, who are your friends?"

"I know who this is," said Promi with a nod at Lorno. "Though I'm not sure," he added wryly, "I know his real name."

"*Nobody* knows my real name yet," said the young man. "Not even me. But you can still call me Lorno."

Shangri smiled at him while she adjusted her kerchief. "Someday, he'll be a famous bard whose name is known all 'round the world."

Promi nodded, then asked Lorno, "So you're still searching for your one great story?"

"Yes," he answered bashfully. "I'm surprised you remember. It's been five whole years since we last spoke with each other."

"That was a day," Promi said sadly, "I will long remember."

Guessing his thoughts, Atlanta insisted, "What happened that day wasn't your fault."

"Then whose fault was it? Everything I did that day has led to disaster!"

"Not everythin'," declared Shangri. She glanced affectionately at Lorno. "At least one person who arrived on that ship was *s'posed* to come here. I'm certain o' that."

Just then, Promi noticed the gleaming ring on her finger. Pointing to it, he asked, "Is that what I think it is?"

Shangri nodded. "'Twas my ma's, long ago."

"And now," Promi said gladly, "it's yours." Both he and Atlanta beamed at their friend.

"It's been yer gift to us, Promi."

"Happy to hear that," he replied. "Just as I was to hear your prayer."

Shangri's eyes sparkled. "An' I was jest as pleased to hear yer reply."

He raised an eyebrow.

"Yes indeed, I heard it jest before I fell asleep."

Promi nodded, thinking, *Good work, Theosor.*

"Well now," said Graybeard, his voice sultry and soothing. "It seems that everyone here knows everyone else except for me."

He bowed politely to Atlanta, which made the knives in his coat clink subtly against each other. "People call me Graybeard. And you must be . . ."

He paused, as if savoring the name. "Atlanta."

"That's right," she replied, indicating the faery on her collar. "And this is my friend Quiggley."

To Atlanta's surprise, the faery emitted a feeling of caution. But she wasn't quite sure. Maybe she'd just misunderstood.

The young man beside her stepped forward. "My name is Promi." He gave Atlanta a brief look. "I'm . . . a visitor."

"Who doesn't come often enough," she added firmly.

Facing Promi, Graybeard gave him a rather stilted bow. It was clear that, for some reason, he was not pleased to have any more company.

"Now that we've all been introduced," said Atlanta, "what are we going to do about that monster?"

"An' the mines," added Shangri. "We still have to stop Reocoles."

Promi nodded grimly. "They're not the only troubles we have to deal with."

"What do ye mean?" asked Shangri.

"I mean," he explained, "that we—"

At that instant, a sudden noise rushed through the forest. Trees all around waved their branches, creaking and snapping furiously, as if struck by a powerful gust of wind. The great willow shook its dangling tresses and twisted its trunk, making a painful moan. It seemed that the entire forest had been shaken by a terrible storm.

Except . . . there was no storm. There wasn't even any wind.

Promi concentrated, trying to listen to whatever the trees might be saying. He started to pick up the first hint of meaning in all the cacophony—when Atlanta shouted.

"Danger!" she cried, grabbing his wrist. "They're warning us of intruders from the spirit realm!"

Quiggley instantly leaped into the air. He sent Atlanta a wave of feeling that combined sheer terror with the sorrow of having lost his whole family to just that kind of intruder. In a flash of blue wings, he disappeared into the forest.

That very second, the trees fell silent. Everything hushed; not even a single leaf on the willow tree stirred.

Then, from a grove of spruces nearby, several dark forms emerged, gliding like deathly shadows. With them came the ominous sound of crackling sparks that burned whatever they touched.

CHAPTER 18

Attack

Mistwraiths!

Six of them approached the group gathered on Moss Island. Eerily floating over the ground, these living blots of darkness crackled viciously, spraying black sparks in their wakes. Whenever a spark hit a trunk or root of the surrounding spruces, it sizzled loudly, like the hiss of a poisonous snake.

Above the companions, the great willow shook its leafy tresses as if telling them to flee. But Atlanta, Promi, and the others stood rigid on the moss, frozen by the mistwraiths' spell of terror.

Promi was the first to break free of the spell. "Atlanta," he barked, "they've come for the Starstone!"

"Right," she agreed, shaking herself as if

waking from a nightmare. "What do we do? How can we stop them?"

The mistwraiths slid closer. Their shadowy folds rippled with satisfaction, and they released another shower of sparks.

Grabbing Atlanta's arm, Promi said, "We *can't* stop them. So you must take it out of its hiding place! Quick, before they get here!"

She hesitated, peering at him quizzically.

"Listen," he urged, "they'll find it when they get here. They can *smell* magic—which they devour as food." He shook her. "Our only hope is to get it first and try to escape!"

Understanding, Atlanta instantly swung around and kneeled by the willow tree's roots. Passing her hands over one especially gnarled root, she whispered urgently in the willow's language, making rhythmic and swishing sounds.

The great tree shuddered, as if protesting. Its long tresses swished loudly.

"Please," begged Atlanta. Again she whispered in the tree's language.

Suddenly, Shangri shouted in alarm. "The trees! On fire!"

Glancing over her shoulder, Atlanta saw that some of the attackers' sparks had ignited a spruce branch. The spruce's resins swiftly fed the flame. In seconds, the whole tree roared in flames. Beside it, another spruce started to catch fire.

All the while, the mistwraiths moved closer. Crackling angrily, they shot sparks in all directions.

Seeing all this, Graybeard silently stepped backward to the other side of the island. Without a word to his companions, he turned, crossed the stream, and slunk into the forest.

Lorno, meanwhile, stepped in front of Shangri. "I'll never let them touch you," he promised.

She shook her head. "But they'll kill ye too. We've got to do somethin' to stop them!"

Her gaze shifted to Promi. "Isn't there anythin' at all ye can do?"

Mind racing, Promi felt heat prickling his chest. Quickly, he glanced over at Atlanta, who was still trying to coax the willow to give up the Starstone. He knew that only seconds remained before the mistwraiths reached them—and then all would be lost.

What can I do? he thought urgently. He couldn't do what he did to that mistwraith at Narkazan's lair—too many of them. And if he used any magic, they'd simply devour it!

Another spruce tree erupted in flames. Columns of thick, dark smoke rose skyward. All the while, the mistwraiths advanced, coming closer and closer.

Suddenly an idea struck Promi. *There's one thing I can do that doesn't need any magic. Just good aim. It won't stop them . . . but it might slow them down.*

Drawing his dagger from its sheath, he hefted the gleaming, translucent weapon in his left hand. Planting his feet firmly in the moss, he drew a steady breath. At the same time, the silver string wrapped securely around his wrist.

Behind him, Atlanta waved her hands furiously over the root. Shangri and Lorno glanced from Promi to the mistwraiths and back again, even as more branches erupted in flames.

Just as the first mistwraith reached the stream, Promi hurled the dagger. It struck one of the burning branches right at its base, slicing clean through the wood. The branch fell downward—but not before Promi, with a sharp twist, tangled it in the silver string. He gave a powerful tug, pulling the flaming branch right on top of the mistwraiths.

Surprised, the dark warriors shrieked and turned around to see who had attacked them from behind. The mistwraith who had been just about to cross the stream released a fountain of sparks and raced back to the flaming spruces, ready for battle against this new threat.

Promi, meanwhile, flicked his arm to free his dagger. The string retracted, drawing the blade back to him. Watching the confused mistwraiths, he slipped the dagger back into its sheath. But he felt only the slightest satisfaction. That ruse had bought them a few more seconds—but it wouldn't work a second time.

He turned back to Atlanta. "Hurry!" he called.

"Now," she pleaded to the willow. "I need it now!"

Meanwhile, the mistwraiths regrouped. Knowing they'd been tricked, they darkened like thunderclouds before a violent storm. Faster than before, they advanced on the island, crackling wrathfully.

Atlanta placed her hands on the gnarled root. "I beg of you, my friend. For the sake of our forest home, for the lives of all the creatures we love, *please* give it to me."

The willow tree twisted, moaning sorrowfully. All at once, the root trembled and then burst out of the ground, clasping the Starstone. The crystal glowed with pure, pulsing light.

Atlanta pulled the crystal free, feeling a sudden rush of magic that made her feel immensely stronger. Just then, the band of mistwraiths reached the stream. Springing to her feet, she started to slip the crystal into the pocket of her gown—when a mistwraith's spark landed on her arm.

"No!" she cried, jerking her arm to get rid of the spark. Fortunately, it had burned through the woven vines of her sleeve but not yet touched her skin. But the jerking motion sent the Starstone flying. It landed on the moss by Shangri's feet.

Instantly, seeing the priceless treasure, the mistwraiths changed course and converged on Shangri. She picked it up, unable to resist marveling at its beauty.

"To me!" shouted Promi, opening his hands wide.

A split second before the first mistwraith reached Shangri, she threw the crystal to Promi. The dark being hissed with frustration and instantly spun around to pursue Promi.

"Run, all of you!" he called. "I'll lead them off."

"Not without me, you won't!" cried Atlanta, running to his side.

Shangri and Lorno did the same. Now all four of them stood together, facing the attackers. Tasting their imminent triumph, the mistwraiths slowed their assault. Crackling with supreme satisfaction, they formed a solid wall of darkness and slid slowly toward their prey, scorching the moss beneath them.

Cradling the Starstone, Promi felt it magnify his magic. But that magic was worthless! If he used it to fight these beings, they would only swallow it and continue unimpeded. What then could he do?

As the line of mistwraiths advanced, the companions backed away slowly. Promi's mind whirled. But he couldn't think of anything. When he and the others reached the edge of the stream, he traded dismal glances with Atlanta. Both of them knew that even if they turned and leaped over the stream and dashed into the woods, the mistwraiths would swiftly hunt them down. Their lives—and the Starstone—would be lost.

The mistwraiths crackled noisily, their shadowy folds rippling with anticipation. Soon, they knew, they would triumph completely. Even if they had to restrain themselves from destroying the son of Sammelvar as their master had commanded, they would certainly capture him . . . as well as the Starstone. And the others? They could kill those mortals with agonizing slowness just for the pleasure of it.

In unison, the mistwraiths advanced. Promi, Atlanta, Shangri, and Lorno stood bravely, but they knew only a few seconds remained. Not only were they about to lose the Starstone, they would also surely lose their lives, their worlds, and all they loved.

The mistwraiths released a huge volley of sparks that landed on the moss right in front of the companions' feet, sizzling viciously. The attackers' forms darkened even more. It was time, at last, to move in for the kill!

Just then a loud roar made the mistwraiths halt. Turning upstream, where the sound was coming from, they saw a lone faery leading an enormous, roaring wall of water. And the water was bearing down on the island like a liquid avalanche.

"Quiggley," shouted Atlanta. "You came back!"

"With help," added Promi.

Powerful help, indeed. For the faery had gone to find the river god himself. Angrier than he'd been in ages to learn that invaders from the spirit realm had dared to come near his beloved waters, Bopaparrúplio whipped up a flash flood with the force of a hundred waterfalls.

Seeing the towering wall of water racing toward them, the mistwraiths screeched in panic. Because this was not magic, just the sheer force of moving water, they couldn't do anything to stop it. They were helpless!

The instant the flood reached the island, it veered out of the stream and narrowed to a highly concentrated jet of water. That jet slammed straight into the mistwraiths, carrying all six of them away. Then the flood rejoined the channel, rushing downstream, bearing the flailing attackers.

Soaked from the spray, the companions cheered and hugged each other in joyful disbelief. Promi, peering downstream at the disappearing torrent, stroked the hilt of his dagger and said quietly, "Thank you, river god."

Beside him, Atlanta nodded in agreement. As Quiggley settled on her shoulder and shook the water off his wings, she smiled at him, adding "And thank *you*, little friend."

Quiggley shrugged his tiny shoulders modestly. But there was no missing the look of true satisfaction on his face.

Turning back to Promi, Atlanta said warily, "They'll come back, of course."

"Sure," he replied with a wink. "But not before we—and the Starstone—are long gone."

CHAPTER 19

Plans

Where exactly," Atlanta asked Promi, "do you think we should go?"

Drenched from the river god's rescue, she squeezed a handful of her hair that was dripping down her neck, wringing some water out of it—being careful, of course, not to give Quiggley another shower. The faery, perched on her shoulder, nodded in approval. Then he removed the hollow berries that served as his shoes, dumping a few drops of water out of each.

Meanwhile, Shangri wrung the water out of her kerchief and tied it again around her frazzled hair, while Lorno inspected the pastries in his pocket to see if they were too soggy to eat. He tasted a hunk of blueberry crumble and smiled, concluding that it tasted every bit as good (and maybe even better) in its moistened state.

The only one of the companions who wasn't doing anything about being soaked was Promi. He was too busy thinking about Atlanta's question. His gaze wandered to the great willow, whose tresses sparkled with spray, studying the gnarled root that had held the magical crystal. That very crystal now rested in his hand, sparkling like a rain-washed star.

At last, he turned back to Atlanta. "I have an answer for you. But," he added with a look of uncertainty, "you might not like it."

She raised an eyebrow. "You've got my attention."

"Well," he began, "I think it's best to get the Starstone away from here. *Far* away."

"The spirit realm?"

"Right. As long as it's here on Atlantis, this whole forest—this whole world—will be in danger." His voice fell to a whisper. "And so will you."

Atlanta bent down, plucked a sprig of sweetstalk fern from the moss, and chewed on the sprig as she considered his idea. Shangri, Lorno, and Quiggley stopped their efforts to dry off, listening closely to the conversation.

"If I take it back to the spirit realm," Promi explained, "your forest home will be less exposed to attackers, at least for a while. Right now, the dangers are everywhere—whether from those mistwraiths or that monster from the mines."

At the mention of that beast, Shangri stiffened. Though her face was unaccustomed to frowning, she did now. "*Everythin'* on Atlantis is in danger as long as that thing be loose."

"True," agreed Promi, "but let's deal with one threat at a time."

"Who knows what that monster's doin' now?" muttered Shangri. "Let's be quick about makin' plans, then go do our best to stop it."

"And Reocoles," added Lorno.

Atlanta nodded. "We will. But first, the Starstone." Peering at

Promi, she said, "If you take it away, the forest is less threatened. But also . . . less magical."

"Just for a while, Atlanta. I'll bring it back here as soon as this war with Narkazan is over."

Heaving a sigh, she replied, "All right. I'll agree to your plan. But *only* on one condition."

"Which is?" asked Promi.

She stepped closer, putting her face so close that their noses nearly touched. "That you'll come back."

"I promise I will."

"Good," she declared. "And don't wait so long that I'll be twice as old as you."

He grinned. "I promise."

Carefully, he placed the Starstone in his pocket. Remembering something, his expression darkened. "While I'm gone," he told her, "don't let that prophecy from Haldor come true! We need Atlantis to survive. And I need *you* to survive."

"What prophecy?" asked Shangri and Lorno in unison.

"That this entire island will be destroyed," said Atlanta grimly. "In what he called *a terrible day and night of destruction.*"

"Maybe," said Shangri worriedly, "that's what the monster's all about."

"We don't know enough to say," answered Atlanta. "But I know who just *might.*"

She glanced at the faery on her shoulder. "Little friend, would you—"

Before she could finish, Quiggley leaped into the air, his luminous wings abuzz, and hovered before her face. He sent her a wave of agreement. For he knew, as she did, that no one understood the events of the forest or its surroundings better than his fellow faeries.

"Thanks," she told him. "Find out whatever you can from your friends that might help us stop this thing."

Instantly, Quiggley flew off. He veered around the old willow like a shot of blue light and disappeared into the woods.

Still anxious, Shangri said, "We can't jest wait here fer him to bring us news."

"Which is why," Atlanta said firmly, "we should go after this beast. Quiggley will find me wherever we are."

"We?" asked Shangri hopefully.

"Yes, we." Atlanta gazed at her. "It's time you and I had another adventure, don't you agree?"

Shangri's smile seemed to light up all of Moss Island.

Lorno, noticing a bulge in Promi's wet tunic, added, "Is that a book you carry?"

"A journal," he replied. "I, er . . . *lost* my old one." He exchanged knowing glances with Atlanta. "It was an old book of dessert recipes, and I liked to scribble in its margins. So Shangri kindly gave me this new one."

He tapped the bulge. "But I don't seem to have enough time anymore to write in it."

Lorno gave an understanding groan. "Writing does take time. And work. And more time. Believe me, I know."

Suddenly he caught his breath. "I almost forgot! Just when the mistwraiths were about to burn us to ashes, right before the river god arrived, I thought of a new name!"

Shangri groaned. "Not again! We both know that whatever name ye pick today ye'll change tomorrow."

"Not this one," he protested. "Trust me, I have a good feeling about this one."

She tousled his hair affectionately. "Jest what is this new name, then?"

He crinkled his nose, enjoying the thought of the name before saying it aloud. Finally, he announced, "My new name is . . . Plato."

Shangri looked uncertain. "Are ye really sure?"

"I am."

"Well," said Promi, "if you want my opinion, stay with Lorno! I mean . . . who would want to read *anything* written by someone named Plato?"

"I might," chimed in Shangri. She gave the young bard a supportive glance. Then she added, "But I think, fer now, I'll still call ye Lorno."

"Whatever you like," he replied, crestfallen. "But I just can't stop feeling that this is the name that will help me find my one great story."

Shangri took both his hands. "Well, all right. Then that's the name I will call ye."

"Really?"

"Yes, Plato."

Seeing his face brighten, she gave his cheek a kiss. Then, releasing his hands, she walked over to Promi. She scrutinized her old friend for a few seconds. When she spoke again, her tone was gravely serious.

"Since yer about to leave us again, don't forget what ye said in yer answer to my prayer."

Promi furrowed his brow. "What did I say?"

"That ye'll never abandon Atlantis. *Never.*"

"You can count on that," he promised. "And do you remember what else I said? About hope?"

Shangri nodded, never breaking eye contact. "Hope has power—more than ye might think."

"Don't forget that." He cocked his head at the young bard. "And don't let him—whatever his name is—forget it, either."

"I won't, Promi." She flung her arms around his broad shoulders. Her voice a whisper, she said, "I'll miss ye while yer gone."

"And I'll miss you too."

Promi turned back to Atlanta, and they simply gazed at each other. Both knew, without saying, what they needed to do now. Yet both felt great resistance to doing it.

Reaching for her hand, Promi led her a few steps away on the soft moss. Somberly, he said, "I don't want to leave you."

Swallowing, she replied, "And I don't want to leave you."

"Remember that time," he said gently, "when we were in that horrible marsh near the Passage of Death?"

She blinked the mist from her eyes. "When we decided that maybe we could be each other's family?"

"Yes." He drew her closer. "Well . . . that's part of what I'm feeling now. But it's, um . . . well, just a small part."

"What," she asked, "is the rest?"

He hesitated, trying to find the right words. It didn't help that Atlanta was looking at him so expectantly, with those beautiful, wide-open eyes of hers. Yet he knew that if there ever was a time to finish that sentence he'd been wanting so badly to say—it was now.

"Atlanta," he began, though for some reason his throat felt impossibly dry. He worked his tongue, but it didn't seem to help. Finally, in a creaky voice, he managed to start again.

"Atlanta, I . . ." His voice trailed off.

She continued to look at him.

"I really . . ."

"Tell me," she encouraged.

He filled his lungs with air. "I really—"

"Well, hello again," called a melodious voice.

Promi and Atlanta both turned to see Graybeard hop across the stream and step onto the island. He scanned the companions, then said bashfully, "I shouldn't have run away like that. It was inexcusable. It was—"

"Cowardly," declared Shangri, glaring at him.

He hung his head. "It was. You're right. I apologize." Then, more brightly, he asked, "Did I miss much?"

"Nothing at all," said Atlanta sarcastically. "Now if you'll just leave us alone . . ." She glanced at Promi, who was pinching his lips together in frustration. "We have things we need to—"

"Accomplish?" interrupted Graybeard, nodding vigorously. "Yes, I know."

Striding over to Atlanta, he pleaded, "Please give me another chance, I beg of you." Placing his hand over his chest, which made his collection of knives bulge slightly under his coat, he vowed, "I will earn back your trust, if you will just let me."

Promi sighed with disappointment. But it wasn't about the man's request. The moment—their moment—had been lost. *All because of my own stupidity,* he raged at himself. *Why do I have to be such a dung-headed dolt?*

"Please," the older man begged Atlanta. "Give me another chance."

Her gaze darted from him to Promi, who seemed so upset it was painful to see, then back again. "All right, all right," she said impatiently, shooing him off as she would a mosquito. She faced Shangri and Plato. "That is, if you both agree."

"I s'pose so," Shangri replied. Directing her next words at Graybeard, she scolded, "But if you don't prove yer worth, we'll send ye packin'."

"Agreed," said the young bard.

"So," asked Graybeard enthusiastically, "where are we going?"

"After that monster you saw," said Atlanta.

Graybeard's enthusiasm faded. "Whatever you say," he mumbled.

"Then we'd better get goin'," Shangri urged. "If that monster is headin' fer the City, it could do terrible damage."

"And if it heads into the forest," observed Atlanta, "the same is true."

"Let's go, then," Shangri said impatiently.

"Right," answered Atlanta. She gave Promi one last look. "Good-bye," she said, her voice catching.

"Good-bye," he echoed. As much as he wanted to say more, he could only gaze at her. After another few heartbeats, he leaped into the sky and vanished from sight.

"Well, I'll be drawn and quartered," said Graybeard in amazement. "I had no idea he could do such a thing! He must be . . ."

"Immortal," said Atlanta, peering up at the sky. "He belongs," she added regretfully, "to another world."

"He'll come back," consoled Shangri. "I'm sure o' that."

Atlanta bit her lip, then lowered her gaze. "I hope so." Drawing a sharp breath, she said, "Anyway, we must go."

"Right," agreed Shangri. "Lead us wherever ye think is best."

"We'll take the short cut to the north side of the forest."

Without another second's delay, Atlanta leaped over the stream and loped into the trees. Shangri and Plato followed, with Graybeard running behind.

If the younger companions had given Graybeard any thought at that moment, they would have guessed that he'd be struggling to keep up with them. On that count, they would have been right. And they would also have assumed that he'd be doubting the wisdom of his plea to join them, maybe even already considering another cowardly exit. But on that count . . . they would have been utterly wrong.

How convenient, he thought as he padded along on the animal track Atlanta had chosen. Holding his coat tightly closed so that none of his knives would fall out, he told himself, *Without that immortal friend of hers around, Atlanta is unprotected. Just as I've been wanting.*

Even as he ran, ducking under branches now and then, he grinned malevolently. *For now I'll let her stay alive so she can lead us out of this miserable forest. And then . . . when I choose just the right moment, I'll finish the job Reocoles hired me to do. And collect that reward he promised!*

He chortled. *But there's no hurry. Choosing the perfect moment takes time. And I always enjoy this part of the process.*

Thinking about the reward, he chortled again. It would be a substantial sum. That was for a very good reason: Good assassins don't come cheap. And he was Zagatash, the very best!

After dealing with Atlanta, he promised himself, he'd savor the treat of dispensing with that sassy redhead and her incompetent friend. As well as that fat old baker, if he got in the way.

Ah, yes, Zagatash thought happily. *I wasn't lying when I told them I'm a kind of entertainer. What I neglected to say is that the person I entertain is me.*

He jumped over a branch that had fallen across the track. *And my favorite entertainment,* he finished, *is killing people.*

Reunited

P romi found his parents and Jaladay just where he'd left them—
on the Universal Bridge. For
them, barely a minute had passed
since Promi's departure to Atlantis. Yet for the
young man, more had happened than could
ever be measured in time.

Sure, I have the Starstone, thought Promi as
he flew toward the group on the glittering
bridge. *But I also have this huge hole in my
heart.*

He frowned, even as Jaladay, sensing his
imminent arrival, turned to face him. *And the
worst part is . . . I dug that hole myself.*

So absorbed in his regrets was he that he
barely noticed the bridge as he approached.
Though it had been built ages earlier, it
remained one of the greatest architectural tri-
umphs of the spirit realm. And it was also, as

Sammelvar had helped Jaladay realize, a powerful visual metaphor of the importance of bridging both light and dark—in life and in oneself.

The brightly lit end, set in the Evarra galaxy, glowed from the radiance of all those bubble worlds in continuous birth, death, and rebirth. Meanwhile, the darkened end, anchored in the Noverro galaxy, throbbed with subtly shifting layers of shadows within shadows. What could be more beautiful?

The ancient poet Dalonna had described the Universal Bridge as "the complete union of night and day." Escholia, who loved poetry as much as anyone, often quoted that line. But her favorite description had been what Jaladay, then only a toddler, had said when she saw it for the first time: "the everything rainbow."

Today, however, all that wondrous beauty and rich meaning was lost on Promi. The only bridge on his mind as he flew toward his family was the one that he sorely wished he could build to connect his life with Atlanta's. Yet that now seemed utterly impossible.

He landed on the bridge only a pace or two away from his parents and sister—as well as the sassy creature who sat on Jaladay's shoulder. Watching Promi set foot on the bridge, Kermi lazily blew a stream of blue bubbles.

"Back so soon!" exclaimed Escholia. She smiled and rushed over to embrace her son. "I always forget how much faster time goes in the mortal realm."

Brushing some of her white hair out of her eyes, she peered at him. "You get more handsome by the day, Promi."

"More stupid, too," grumbled Kermi.

"Hush, now," said Jaladay, giving the kermuncle's long tail a sharp tug. "A little manners would help."

"Harrumph. So would a little intelligence."

Promi's father smiled, giving even more wrinkles to his careworn face. "Good to see you again, my son. We are grateful you're unharmed."

Stepping closer, Sammelvar asked, "What news of the Starstone?"

Before Promi could even open his mouth to reply, Jaladay pointed at his tunic pocket. "He brought it back with him."

Promi scowled at her. "With a sister like you," he teased, "nobody gets to deliver any news."

She grinned. "True, but this way we get the news accurately."

Kermi chuckled, swinging his tail so it rapped against her arm.

"Tell us more," urged Sammelvar.

"Yes, do," pleaded Escholia. The ocean-glass crystal she wore around her neck glowed with anticipation.

Reaching into his tunic, Promi pulled out the treasured crystal. It rested in the palm of his hand, surprisingly small for something so powerful. Suddenly, all the prisms embedded in the bridge's cables glowed more brightly. The entire bridge swelled in radiance—something that hadn't seemed remotely possible a few seconds before.

Escholia gasped in amazement. "The bridge!"

"The Starstone," said her husband admiringly. "It has lost none of its awesome power."

"How did you get it?" asked Jaladay. She paused to gaze at the brilliant colors surrounding them on the bridge, despite the turquoise band that covered her eyes. "Tell us the whole story."

"Don't you know already?" asked Promi. "Seer that you are?"

"Sure," she said smugly. "But this will give you the illusion of knowing something I don't already know."

Sammelvar smirked at his wife of so many years. "You give me that illusion all the time."

Playfully, Escholia shoved his shoulder. "Just to keep you in line."

"You succeed every time," he replied as he gazed at her lovingly.

She said nothing, but her ocean-glass amulet glowed even brighter than before.

Sammelvar's expression turned more serious. Facing Promi, he asked, "Did you encounter any mistwraiths?"

He nodded grimly. "Six of them. And they would have destroyed us for sure, if the river god hadn't come to our rescue."

The elder spirit grinned slightly. "Good old Bopaparrúplio. I always regretted his choice to leave the spirit realm to live among mortals . . . but I'm glad he was there to help."

Escholia chuckled softly. "I've always liked that his name sounds like a bubbling stream, if you say it fast enough."

"So," said Sammelvar proudly. "You accomplished your goal!"

Promi's expression darkened. "Only part of it."

His parents looked at him quizzically.

Putting the Starstone back in his pocket, he explained, "Yes, we kept the crystal out of Narkazan's hands." He blew a long, dejected breath. "But when it came to Atlanta . . . I was an absolute and complete idiot."

"Very good," said Kermi, clapping enthusiastically. "Now she knows you for who you really are. That's the foundation of any successful relationship."

Jaladay gave his tail another tug. "Shhh," she commanded. "Show some compassion."

"I will when he shows some *sense*." The kermuncle folded his tiny arms across his chest and blew a new stream of bubbles.

Promi scanned the faces of his family morosely. "I had my chance to tell her I really love her. And then I totally ruined it."

His mother gently stroked his cheek. "I understand, Promi. Nothing hurts more than missing the chance to say you love someone." She smiled warmly. "That's why I sang to you in your dreams all those years we were apart."

Sammelvar nodded. "And we love you very much, son."

"That goes for all of us," added Jaladay.

On her shoulder, Kermi just rolled his eyes.

Promi looked at them, his reunited family, with gratitude. What a blessing to have them all in his life. They deserved to hear him say that more often than he'd done in the past.

His gaze took in, for the first time this visit, the remarkable bridge where they stood. Linking a radiantly colorful cluster of worlds with a richly dark one, the Universal Bridge held the full spectrum of possibilities. Just as he himself did.

He stood a bit taller. Somehow, this bridge reminded him that darkness and light exist in everyone. Including himself. And that, just like his family, Atlanta most likely understood that point.

Even so, he promised himself, *I'm going to get back down there as soon as this war is over—and tell her once and for all!*

Jaladay, who had heard his thought, nodded. Telepathically, she told him, *I do believe you will.*

Suddenly she gasped. She leaned over the vaporstone railing, peering fearfully into the shadows of the bridge's dark side.

"Attack!" she cried—just as a bolt of immense energy smashed into the middle of the bridge.

CHAPTER 21

Anguish

The Universal Bridge rocked violently as the attack's thunderous boom echoed across the realm. Vaporstone struts and railings in the bridge's midsection exploded, hurling debris into the air. Several cables snapped, whipping wildly, while others twisted from the added strain.

"Flashbolt!" shouted Sammelvar. "Scatter, everyone! Before they send another—"

Boom! His command came too late. A second blast, shot from somewhere in the darkness of the Noverro galaxy, slammed into the bridge. Hit by the flashbolt—the most powerful weapon in the spirit realm, capable of destroying even the strongest immortals with a direct hit—more of the midsection exploded, severing cables and casting debris everywhere.

Promi and Jaladay tumbled backward onto

the buckling bridge, colliding with broken struts on the walkway. When Jaladay hit, Kermi bounced off her shoulder. Screeching, Kermi fell over the side and plunged downward.

Escholia stumbled over to Sammelvar. Desperately, she searched her husband's face. "What do we do?"

His gaze darted to their children, still on their backs. Promi was wrestling to lift a huge broken strut off his leg, while Jaladay lay stunned from the impact. Both were helpless if another blast should hit that spot.

Facing Escholia, he declared, "You should fly! Now—before another blast. I'll stay long enough to protect them!"

Seeing that Promi and Jaladay were so exposed, she shook her head. "Then I'll stay too."

"No! You must leave!"

Deep clarity came to Escholia's face. "You may be the leader of the spirit realm, but I make my own decisions. I'm *staying*."

Sammelvar sighed in defeat. "All right, then. Help me make them a sphere."

Placing her hands on top of his, Escholia said firmly, "This is right." But the ocean-glass crystal on her neck swiftly darkened until it showed no trace of light at all.

Boom! Another flashbolt smashed into the bridge. One of the immense support towers, holding hundreds of cables, buckled. It teetered directly above Promi and Jaladay, creaking and wobbling precariously.

The two elder spirits, nearly knocked over by the blast, managed to keep their hands together. They concentrated on their task—even as nearby cables snapped and vaporstone struts burst apart beside them.

The whole bridge twisted, breaking more cables. Listing dangerously to one side, the once-elegant structure groaned from the growing stress. Above Promi and Jaladay, the support tower finally broke off and collapsed toward them.

At the same instant, a powerful burst of blue light flowed out of the hands of Sammelvar and Escholia, streaming toward their children. Just a split second before the tower fell on top of them, the blue light coalesced into a transparent sphere that completely surrounded them.

As the tower crashed down, the sphere burst out of the wreckage. Gleaming from the light of the Evarra galaxy, it spun as it flew away from the bridge.

Escholia's misty blue eyes met her husband's golden ones. "They're safe," she panted. A tiny spark of light returned to her amulet.

Sammelvar looked at her with all the love and loyalty of so many years together. "Yes. Now we must—"

Another flashbolt struck the bridge right where they stood, swallowing them in an explosion of debris. The destabilized bridge twisted more violently than ever.

At the same time, Promi and Jaladay both sat upright in the sphere. Instantly, they realized what their parents had done—even as they witnessed the new blast strike the spot where they'd been standing.

"No!" cried Jaladay, putting her hands on both sides of her head and shaking in anguish. *"Please, no!"*

"Not them!" shouted Promi, watching the flashbolt hit. He peered at the dust and debris from the strike, hoping against hope that they had somehow survived.

The debris cleared, revealing a gaping hole in the body of the bridge. And in the entire realm, as well. For Escholia, the spirit of grace, and Sammelvar, the spirit of wisdom, had both perished.

As Promi and Jaladay watched, the bridge finally gave way. The remaining towers fell, smashing onto the walkway. Cables flew, struts burst, and with a terrible convulsion, the whole structure collapsed.

Fragments drifted down into the twin galaxies below—one radiant with light, the other cloaked with darkness. Some of those pieces glowed bright before vanishing; others fell into eternal night.

Seconds later, nothing remained of the Universal Bridge— nothing but a great empty space in the sky.

Promi and Jaladay could only watch in stunned silence. Then, embracing each other tightly, they wept the most bitter tears of their lives. And then they wept some more.

CHAPTER 22

A Well-Deserved Bath

After a long and difficult day of barking at his servants at the temple, the Divine Monk sank peacefully into his bath. As hot water poured into the tub from the specially designed golden faucet given to him by his most capable subject, the great inventor Reocoles, the Divine Monk beamed with pleasure. That made all of his multiple chins turn upward, giving the impression of a stack of smiles rising up from his collarbone.

The day's indignities—his scarlet robe's buttons had burst when he tried to bend over, for the third time that week—began to melt away. Gradually, the spiritual leader of the City of Great Powers relaxed. Clouds of steam rose from the bath, obscuring the painted tiles showing earlier Divine Monks performing various miracles and acts of heroism.

He sank lower in the tub, careful not to get any water on his gold turban, studded with diamonds and an enormous ruby in its center. Positioning himself comfortably, he could feel the warm water rising toward his shoulders. It didn't matter if the bottom of his thin white beard, decorated with precious jewels, got wet—the servants could dry that off when he was done. Same with his toe rings, finger rings, and multiple bracelets.

Most of his body would soon be submerged—except, of course, for his swollen belly, which lifted above the water like a whale at sea. But he had a solution for that.

"Towel!" he commanded.

Immediately, two white-robed male servants darted into the room and carefully draped a heated towel over the mound of his belly. After sprinkling the towel with fragrant rosewater, they bowed low and backed away.

Before they reached the door, however, the Divine Monk growled, "It's not even, you fools. Fix it!"

Darting back into the steamy room, the servants bowed again and said in unison, "Whatever you command, He Who Has Been Kissed by the Wisdom of Immortal Spirits."

"Forget the niceties," came the command from the tub. "Fix the towel!"

Quickly, they slid the towel slightly to one side so that it covered the whole mound.

"Good," barked the Divine Monk. "Now in a few more seconds, when the tub is completely full, turn off the faucet. Then leave me in peace."

Anxiously, the two men bowed again and said, "As you wish, Holy Wondrous Eternally Blessed Master."

As they stood by the door, the supreme leader sighed deeply.

No one, he thought, *has ever deserved a hot bath more than I do today.*

Suddenly, his feet felt something utterly wrong. And totally unexpected.

"The water!" he bellowed. "It's cooling down!"

The pair of servants rushed over. Frantically, they both tried to turn the faucet for more hot water.

"Make it hot!" cried the Divine Monk, waving his arms in the air. "*Now,* you imbeciles."

Desperately, the servants wrenched the handle of the faucet, turning it as far as it would go. Suddenly—the handle broke off.

Water—cold water—erupted like a geyser. Spraying everyone and everything in the room, the fountain of water couldn't be stopped.

Now completely outraged, the Divine Monk roared, "Get me out of here! Quickly, before I drown!"

As he tried to sit up, his soggy turban slid off and fell into the tub with a splash. "Baboons' bowels!" he cursed. "Just wait until I tell that fool Reocoles what I think of his inventions."

Water sprayed relentlessly as the servants tried to pull their master out of his bath. Unfortunately, in all the commotion, he'd wedged his plump body so securely into the tub that he couldn't be budged.

"Get me out of here!" he bellowed, struggling to free himself.

But the tub clung to his body like the shell of an overweight turtle. The servants pulled and pried while their supreme leader cursed and beat his hands against the tub. Meanwhile, ice-cold water poured over all of them.

"Out of here!" shouted the Divine Monk. "I don't care how, but get me free of this!"

Abruptly, the wall adjacent to the temple's outer courtyard cracked. The beam holding up the ceiling buckled, splitting numerous painted tiles. Caught by surprise, the plump monk and his servants froze.

"What in the name of the immortal spirits is happening?" cried the Divine Monk. "I didn't give permission for any of this!"

At that instant, the entire courtyard wall crumbled. Completely naked, stuck inside his bathtub, the supreme ruler of the City found himself facing—

"A monster!" he wailed.

Like his petrified servants, the Divine Monk stared into the gaping jaws of a beast that resembled a gigantic yellow toad. Then, faster than the blink of an eye, the toad's massive tongue shot out and wrapped around both the monk and his tub. As the monk screamed in terror, the tongue drew him deep into a mouth that gurgled with poisonous slime.

CHAPTER 23

Screams

Before they even reached the gates to the City, they heard the screams.

Atlanta led the way, just as she had through the forest, running across the stretch of packed dirt that led to the wide bridge before the gates. Following close behind came Shangri, her kerchief again dangling from a few strands of red hair after being clipped by several branches. Right after her ran Plato, formerly Lorno—though he continued to insist that this new name would last. Last of all jogged Zagatash, a few stray leaves caught in his gray beard . . . and a dangerous look in his eyes.

As they arrived at the bridge, they all noticed the considerable damage it had sustained. Wooden planks lay broken everywhere, crushed by something enormously heavy. Guardrails had been shoved aside, pushed into the deep canyon of the Deg Boesi. Far below, the river frothed and pounded as it raced through the channel, its banks littered with broken debris from the bridge.

Carefully, the companions picked their way across, doing their best to avoid stepping on any planks too weak to hold their weight. Atlanta easily maneuvered across, trotting and leaping with the grace of a gazelle. Shangri and Plato found the going much more tricky—and once the young bard stepped on a plank that splintered right under him, nearly pitching him into the canyon.

Surprisingly, the man they called Graybeard moved with great agility across the bridge. Benefiting from a lifetime of practice as an assassin, he moved swiftly and silently, closing the gap between himself and the younger members of the group. As he padded over the bridge, he continued to hold his coat closed to make sure none of his knives jiggled loose.

The time for my blades will come, he told himself. *Soon enough.*

There was no need to rush, he knew from experience. The opportunity to skewer his prey, in this case Atlanta, always presented itself in time. Just as his brutal father had waited for the right moment to slice him with a kitchen knife when he was a young boy—leaving him with scars across his cheek and chin that he could hide only by growing a thick beard.

All he needed to do, Zagatash understood, was to stay alert and poised for action. Until then . . . he could savor, as he always did, the joy of the hunt. The feeling of growing anticipation. The certainty that he would, once again, be fully in control, wielding his own deadly blades, carving his own painful scars.

Eyeing Atlanta as she gave Shangri a hand getting off the bridge, he clucked with satisfaction. *Now you are so lithe and pretty, so full of confidence! That will soon change.*

Together, the four of them strode up to what remained of the gates to the City. Torn completely off their hinges, the gates had been smashed to splinters. Their massive posts had been snapped in half as if they'd been no stronger than twigs. And the whole area reeked of yellow slime that smelled worse than rotting carcasses. Frantic people, some dragging gravely wounded family and friends, struggled past as they tried to leave the settlement.

"Are ye mad?" one elderly woman called to Shangri. "Yer goin' the wrong way!"

Shangri just clenched her jaw and pushed ahead. She hoped with all her heart that her father, whom she'd left at his bakery that very morning, was unharmed.

Screams shattered the air constantly. Along with those screams came a steady din of other sounds—walls collapsing, windows breaking, and frightened animals braying or shrieking. Plus, once in a while, the howling bellow of the monster.

Smoke rose from all parts of the City. From the market square, a towering cloud lifted skyward. Even through the sooty haze that clung to the Machines District—a fact of life since the arrival of Reocoles—the companions saw billowing smoke from buildings on fire. Yet the darkest clouds, and the loudest screams, seemed to come from a different part of the City.

The temple of the Divine Monk.

Following the trail of rancid slime that led down the cobblestone streets to the temple, the companions passed many more wounded people. One man sat, his head in his hands, sobbing uncontrollably. Nearby, a woman stood in shock, facing the pile of rubble that was all that remained of her mud-brick home, standing amidst shards of glass and a tangled line of laundry. And a grieving father and mother, bending over the body of a child who had been crushed by a fallen chimney, wailed piteously.

Even as they pressed ahead toward the temple, Shangri wanted to break away and see if her father was safe. But she guessed he could probably take care of himself—and she knew the most important thing to do now was to try to stop the monster.

But how? The companions racked their brains for an answer. Whatever the means, they knew they needed to end this beast's savagery—or Atlantis itself could not survive.

No less than the others, Zagatash wanted that beast eliminated. He grimaced, hopping over a puddle of slime. *Who,* he wondered, *would have any need for an assassin if everything was collapsing in ruin?* Such devastation was bad for business. An assassin thrived on stability—hirings came from ambitious people who wanted to gain power or greedy people who wanted to gain wealth. Or, in the case of Reocoles, someone who wanted both.

Maybe I'll let her live a little longer, thought Zagatash. *To see if she's clever enough to find some way to destroy that beast.*

As the companions neared the temple, they were nearly run over by a group of half-crazed monks and priestesses, their tan robes splattered with mud, as well as blood. Screaming and waving their arms wildly, the temple's residents fell over themselves to escape. The exodus swelled still more as Atlanta and the others arrived at the temple gates.

Facing the tide of panicked people, Shangri shook her head in disbelief. She barely recognized the calm and stately entrance to the City's spiritual heart. This was a place she'd known her whole life—the tranquil spot where she'd often delivered freshly baked pastries and pies! Now, by contrast, it was the scene of more tumult than the stampede of goats, horses, and people through the market square she'd seen on the day, years ago, when she first met Promi.

As they pushed through the crowd at the entrance, all four companions abruptly halted. The temple's main courtyard thronged with panicking, injured people—along with piles of smoking rubble that only hours before had stood as ornately crafted buildings. Broken balconies, split gilded beams, and smashed statues of immortal spirits lay everywhere. So did countless fragments of brightly colored tiles, turquoise stonework, and stained glass windows.

On top of that, the temple's great bell tower, a fixture of the City for centuries, looked severely damaged. A gaping hole had opened in one sidewall, while deep fissures ran all the way up to the copper dome over the bell. It looked so precarious that one strong gust of wind could knock the whole thing over.

Squatting in the center of all this wreckage was the beast who had caused so much damage. Swollen from everything it had devoured that day, it looked nearly twice its original size. Its tongue and teeth had swelled in proportion. Even the festering lumps on its back had grown to be as big as anvils.

Yet even so, the monster hungered for more. Driven to consume endlessly, it needed to eat to sustain its enormous bulk—as well as what it carried. For it carried something very precious both to itself and to Narkazan.

Aghast, the companions could only watch as the gargantuan attacker slammed its great bulk against the outer wall of the Divine Monk's personal residence. The wall split open, buckled, and fell into the courtyard with a thunderous crash.

"No!" shrieked Shangri, as the toadlike monster's terrible tongue shot out and wrapped around the Divine Monk himself.

Caught in the midst of taking a bath (which, Shangri assumed, he had earned after a long day of ministering to the sick and needy), the Divine Monk squealed and waved his arms helplessly. But the tongue drew him—as well as his tub—swiftly into the monster's mouth. As the jaws closed, Shangri heard the sickening crunch of breaking bones and tile work. Right away, a large bulge moved down the beast's bloated gullet.

"Sweet puddin' o' the gods!" cried a familiar voice behind them.

Just as Shangri turned, her father's powerful arms wrapped around her. Holding her tight, he swayed from side to side.

"I be fine, Papa," she cried. "That is, if ye don't crush me to death."

"By the everlastin' gods," panted Morey, "I wasn't sure I'd see ye again."

He set her down. Peering at her, he said, "Now it's time we get out o' this cursed place. While we still can!"

Shangri placed her hands on her hips. "No, Papa. We here—" She gestured at the group. "We're resolved to try an' stop this monster. Fer good."

"Then yer resolved to die," he objected. "Look at that hulkin' beast! Nobody short o' the gods is goin' to succeed."

"We have to try," chimed in Atlanta, stepping to Shangri's side. "For the sake of this island."

Very good, thought Zagatash, stroking his beard. *You take care of the beast . . . and then I'll take care of you.*

"I feel the same way," declared Shangri.

"Me too," announced Plato.

Glancing over at the hulking beast in the courtyard, Morey sighed. "All right, then. I can see there's no changin' yer minds." Shifting his gaze to Atlanta, he said, "Ye must be Shangri's friend from the forest."

"I am. And you must be her father."

"That I am. Thank ye fer what ye've done to help her stay alive." With another glance at the monster, he added, "So far."

Morey sucked in his breath, then declared, "Given all this mess, there's only one thing left fer me to do."

"What, Papa?"

The baker locked gazes with his daughter. "Join ye! What else?"

Shangri wrapped her arms around the burly man. Then, pulling away, she quickly retied her kerchief and asked, "But exactly what are we goin' to do?"

Morey shook his head, sending up a puff of flour. "That I don't know. That beast looks so fierce it'd survive almost anythin'."

"Almost!" cried Plato excitedly. "I have an idea. Follow me!"

Dodging the fleeing monks and priestesses, he led them over to the bell tower. With the gaping hole at its base, it seemed to be ready to fall down at any moment. Even as they stood there, a new crack opened under the copper dome.

Guessing Plato's plan, Morey said, "Ye can't be serious, lad. If we try to push this tower over on top o' the beast, it'll be *us* who gets buried under all that stone."

"Which is why," the young man replied, "we're not going to do that."

Puzzled, Morey scratched his head. "So what's yer plan?"

Scanning the faces of the group, Plato declared, "*We* won't topple this tower." He pointed at the toadlike beast, now finishing his meal of the Divine Monk's unlucky pair of servants. "But that thing will!"

Atlanta brightened. "Good thinking! Let's do whatever it takes—"

"To get that beast's attention," finished Shangri.

"All right," agreed Morey, still uncertain.

The baker bent down and grabbed a large stone from the tower's broken base. Rearing back, he heaved it at the monster. But the stone merely bounced off the lumps on its back and rolled into the courtyard. The beast didn't even seem to notice, continuing to gulp down the remains of the Divine Monk's bathroom fixtures.

Frowning, the baker said, "Well then, let's try doin' it all together."

"Good idea," said Plato.

Immediately, the companions started searching for something each of them could throw. All except Zagatash. He quietly slunk behind the tower, well out of harm's way. No reason to risk his throwing arm—or his life—on this harebrained scheme.

Besides, he thought gleefully, *whether or not their plan works, this is exactly the moment I've been waiting for.*

With the supreme confidence of a skilled assassin, he reached into his coat and drew out a knife. Twirling it in his hand, he watched the blade flash in the light. He kissed the blade gently— his ritual that always meant someone's life was about to end.

CHAPTER 24

Collapse

By now, all the surviving monks and priestesses had escaped the temple grounds. No one remained save the companions—and the monster whose hunger for destruction seemed boundless.

Atlanta, completely unaware that Zagatash was at that very moment preparing to hurl his knife at her back, picked up the head of a smashed statue. Catching her breath, she realized that it had been a statue of Escholia, the goddess who so personified a life of grace.

Promi's mother, she thought, cradling the marble head in her hands.

Addressing the goddess herself, she whispered, "I hope you are well, even in this terrible time in the spirit realm." Peering into the eyes of the severed head, she added, "And I pray your son will survive whatever is to come."

She checked on the others and saw that Shangri and Plato had also picked up hefty pieces of statues. Morey hefted another stone from the bell tower's base, even bigger than the one he'd thrown before. Atlanta looked around for their gray-bearded companion, but he was nowhere in sight. *Most likely,* she concluded, *he has fled again.*

Hidden by the bell tower, Zagatash peeked around the corner and watched Atlanta. "Draw your last few breaths," he muttered.

The monster, whose swollen girth filled at least a third of the courtyard, gulped down the last of the Divine Monk's bathroom fixtures (as well as the leg of one of the servants that had been bitten off earlier). Rivers of yellow slime dripped from its jaws, as its tongue probed the ground for whatever was left to devour.

Suddenly—one of the swollen lumps on its back fell off. Landing with a *squelch,* it rolled to a stop. Then, out of the gelatinous membrane that surrounded it . . . something emerged. Something that resembled a gigantic slug—dismal yellow in color, with dark holes for eyes and a wide mouth.

Seeing this, Atlanta and her companions gasped in unison. Only Graybeard, who hadn't seen what had happened, didn't react. But for the others, the sight was a horrible shock.

Offspring, Atlanta told herself in disbelief. *The monster's offspring!*

At that moment, the monster lumbered over and licked the newborn with its tongue, drooling yellow slime all over its small body. In response, the offspring squealed and waddled away. Spying the body of a dead priestess, it immediately started gnawing on the woman's face and neck. Bones crunched and blood spurted, but the offspring went right on eating.

Atlanta, like the others, winced at this gruesome sight. Then she noticed one crucial difference between the big and small beasts: the pair of ragged, leathery appendages on the offspring's back. Wings!

So it can fly, Atlanta realized. *Anywhere on Earth.*

Swallowing hard, she took in the importance of this discovery. *Soon everywhere in the world, these monsters will be wreaking all the same havoc as here!*

Studying the big monster's back, she could tell, without doubt, that several more of the swollen lumps were nearly ready to fall off. Already, one of them was wriggling inside its membrane—eager to feed itself on mortal flesh.

"Let's try to get them all with our plan!" she called to Shangri, Plato, and Morey. "It's our best chance!"

Waving to the others to come closer, she urged, "Come, stand together. Right here in front of the tower."

As the others gathered around her, she cast a glance upward. The tower looked so fragile that it almost seemed to sway on its crumbling foundation. Another crack split open near the top, dropping a chunk of mortar that fell to the courtyard, barely missing Morey's shoulder.

"After we get the big one's attention," Atlanta said, "stay right where you are until the last possible second."

The others nodded.

Spying the leg of a broken statue nearby, Atlanta thought of something else. Positioning herself in front of the others, she said, "If it uses that tongue, I'll deal with it. Just stay here long enough to make it charge us."

Plato gulped, staring at the toadlike behemoth. "Be careful what you wish for."

Shangri, by his side, whispered, "I'm wishin' we get out o' this alive."

"Ready to throw?" asked Atlanta.

Behind her Zagatash slipped out of hiding and positioned himself. Raising his knife, he quietly answered, "Yes, I most certainly am."

"Now!" shouted Atlanta.

Together, she and her companions hurled their weighty objects. All of them struck the beast's back. But as before, it didn't even seem to notice.

Then Morey's stone bounced across its back, struck its shoulder, and fell into one of its eyes of utter blackness. The beast suddenly roared in outrage. It whirled around, slamming its vast bulk into a temple fountain that instantly crumbled.

Seeing four mortals nearby, it shot out its tongue. Like a huge snake, the tongue reached across the courtyard at the young woman who stood closest.

Atlanta, though, was ready. Even as the monster spun around, she grabbed the leg of the statue off the ground. Moving with amazing speed, she lifted it like a bat—and swung.

Just as the tongue almost struck, the bat slammed into it, knocking it aside. The monster bellowed in pain—as well as rage. Furious at this unexpected challenge, it reared up on its stubby hind legs. Then it charged, hurtling toward its prey.

As the beast barreled toward them, Atlanta traded glances with her companions. All held steady . . . while the monster charged closer.

And closer.

And closer.

"Now!" cried Atlanta, leaping aside.

All the others did the same, throwing their bodies as far out of the beast's path as they could. An instant later—

Slam! The monster plowed straight into the base of the temple tower.

Slightly dazed, the beast stood still for an instant, trying to ascertain what had just happened. Right then, the entire tower collapsed, burying the monster—as well as its offspring—under a mountainous mass of stone.

As the structure crashed down, the copper dome slammed onto the stones. The temple bell, whose resonant sound had called the faithful to prayers for centuries, rang one last time.

The bell's reverberations filled the courtyard. As that sound died away, another one rose in its place: the companions' jubilant cheers.

Only one person in the courtyard wasn't cheering. Zagatash, who had realized at the last instant that he was standing too close when the tower collapsed, picked himself up from the pile of rubble where he'd leaped just in time to avoid injury. Though he'd survived just fine, he wasn't thinking about that right now. All his attention had returned to his prey.

As he brushed the mortar dust off his coat, he spoke silently to Atlanta. *Good work ridding us of that beast. Now . . . I have a present for you.*

With satisfaction, he eyed his target. She was still within easy throwing range—and still utterly unaware of the danger. Just as Atlanta opened her arms to give Shangri a hug of congratulations, the assassin pulled a new knife from his coat, planted his feet, and threw.

"We did it!" shouted Shangri joyfully.

"Oh, Shang—" Atlanta started to say. Suddenly, her face froze with a look of pain. She fell forward into her friend's arms.

"What?" wondered Shangri, alarmed. Then, seeing the knife buried in Atlanta's back, she screamed.

CHAPTER 25

Shangri's Prayer

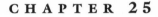

Morey and Plato rushed over. "No!" they both shouted at once, their voices joining Shangri's wails of anguish as she held the limp body of Atlanta.

All around them lay rubble from the destroyed temple. Broken beams, crushed statues, shattered glass, and smashed mortar lay everywhere. But all the companions could think about was something far more valuable that might also have been destroyed—the life of their friend.

Meanwhile, Zagatash chortled mirthfully as he slipped out of the temple grounds. "At last, another job done," he congratulated himself, giving his coat a pat. "Now it's time to collect that payment."

Blood seeped rapidly from Atlanta's wound, which was right behind her heart, staining her gown of woven vines. The vines' purple color darkened by the second.

Gently, they set her down on the ground. Furrowing his brow, Morey said to the others, "Forgive me, but I've got to do this. Fer her sake."

With great care, he withdrew the weapon from Atlanta's back. Blood soaked the blade all the way up to the hilt. Growling angrily, Morey said, "This belonged to that stranger Graybeard! I should never have let him sweet-talk his way into yer group."

Shangri bit her lip, staring down at Atlanta. The woodswoman's normally ruddy complexion was fast turning pale. And blood continued to pour from her wound.

"It's not yer fault, Papa. But what," she asked, fighting back a sob, "can we do now?"

Morey tossed aside the knife in disgust, then pulled off his baker's apron. Swiftly, he wrapped it around Atlanta's torso like a big white bandage.

Just then they heard a deep, anguished groan from under the pile of rubble where the tower had collapsed. Trading frightened glances, they immediately grabbed Atlanta, lifted her off the ground, and dashed toward the temple gates.

The instant they passed out of the grounds, the mountain of rubble exploded. Stones rained down, smashing into the remaining buildings and shattering stained glass. The copper dome flew into the air like a huge metallic bird before it crashed into the remains of the Divine Monk's residence. The old bell tumbled aside—but rather than ringing again, it cracked into two pieces, making a low moan that filled the courtyard.

The moment the companions ducked into a small alley, the monster smashed out of the temple gates. Shaking the debris off its hulking body, it roared with all the wrath that boiled inside it.

The walls of the nearby buildings trembled with the violence of that roar.

Possessed by such rage, the monster didn't even notice that its newborn offspring had also survived. Already, the small beast had returned to devouring what remained of the priestess who was its first meal. Nor did the monster notice that, as it tore through the temple gates, two more offspring fell off its back. Right away, they pulled themselves out of their membranes and started hunting for food.

Setting down Atlanta with great care, the group kneeled by her side, remaining perfectly quiet so the monster wouldn't hear them. Yet Shangri and Plato both felt that their hearts were thumping so loud, they'd surely be discovered.

Morey, meanwhile, peered at the fallen young woman. Already, his apron was soaked through with blood. He bent low, listening for her breathing. Only the faintest whisper of a breath could be heard . . . and that was fading fast.

Angrily, the big monster sniffed the air. Then, spewing slime from its cavernous mouth, it roared again.

Suddenly it hesitated. Rotating its head toward the alley where the group was hiding, it sniffed again, catching a familiar smell.

The companions remained as still as stones, afraid to move the slightest little bit. Beads of sweat rolled down Morey's brow.

All at once, the monster grunted and sprang down the cobblestone street, heading away from the companions. Raging, it slammed its massive bulk against one building, bringing down the whole façade. Another of its offspring fell off its back and landed on the street. The beast continued on its rampage, crushing abandoned wagons and pulverizing anything in its path.

As it happened, not far down that same street, Zagatash stood holding a knife to the throat of one very frightened man who stood backed up against the wall of a building. The assassin pressed his blade against the trembling man's skin.

"The time has come to pay your debts, Reocoles! Now hand over my reward."

"G-g-gladly," said the master machinist. "But I don't carry that much money with me. We'll have to go back to my building to get it."

Seeing Zagatash's look of distrust, Reocoles continued, "Look here, I only left my building because someone on the Divine Monk's staff ran over and told me that his Excellency was having trouble with his bathwater."

"He's having more trouble than that," hissed Zagatash. "But no more talk. I want my payment! So take me to your building. And no tricks, now. Or your life is over."

"No tricks!" Heaving with relief as the killer removed the blade, Reocoles promised, "You will get all the payment you deserve."

Just then—the building under which they stood suddenly crashed down on top of them. Neither of them even had a chance to scream before they died, crushed completely under a mountain of rubble.

Lurching past, the monster roared so loudly that several chimneys toppled from neighboring buildings and smashed down on the street. The raging beast's fevered brain held only one thought, aside from continuing to eat—to find those people who had tricked it into toppling that bell tower. And to make sure they suffered greatly before they died.

Back in the alley where they were hiding, those very same people huddled over Atlanta's body. Although the monster had moved away, Shangri, Plato, and Morey felt no joy in escaping. Her face twisted in pain, Shangri looked down at their fallen friend.

"We must help her," she said hoarsely. "An' quick."

"Sure," agreed Plato. "But how?"

Morey mopped his brow with his sleeve. Dejectedly, he said, "No one can help her now, I fear. No one . . . but the gods."

Shangri suddenly stiffened. "I know who can help!" she cried. "If I can jest reach him in time."

Without another second's delay, she stood and dashed down the alley. Her feet slapped on the cobblestones as she raced ahead, veered into another street, and leaped over a broken window box that held a single, dying daffodil.

Running through the market square—completely empty, with unattended stalls of fruit, leather goods, musical instruments, and handmade jewelry—Shangri veered again down a darkened alley. Seconds later, she burst into the light. Puffing with exhaustion, she darted over to the rickety, unfinished bridge over the river gorge.

The Bridge to Nowhere.

From every post and line of rope, prayer leaves fluttered. Shangri ran onto the bridge, even though it creaked and swayed under her weight. On all sides, the leaves inscribed with blessings and prayers—messages to loved ones who had died, hopes for a better life, songs of praise to the spirit realm—trembled in the vaporous wind.

At the very end of the bridge, she stepped across a gaping hole and stood on the outermost plank. Far below her, at the bottom of the canyon, the mighty river surged on its way to the sea, pounding relentlessly. Clouds of mist spiraled all around her—mist that, she knew, held wind lions who carried people's prayers to the spirit realm.

She moved as close to the edge as she could possibly go, wrapping her toes around the end of the plank. Opening her arms wide, she called with all her heart—to the mist, to the wind lions, and to one dear friend who was so very far away.

"Promi! Hear me, please—if you can possibly hear my voice callin' all the way from yer bridge."

She started to go on, then her sobs came pouring out. Tears streamed down her cheeks. Somehow, amidst the sobs, she forced herself to go on.

"She's dyin', Promi. Atlanta is dyin'!"

Fighting back more tears, she called into the swirling vapors. "Come help her, Promi! Come help her before there's no more hope."

Shangri hung her head. Her kerchief, loosened from her mad dash through the City, slipped off completely. It fell, catching wind currents, into the gorge, spiraling downward. Finally, it vanished in the mist.

"I'm tryin' to do what ye told me," she whispered, so softly that she could hardly hear her own words. "Tryin' to keep some hope."

She swallowed the lump in her throat. "But it's hard, Promi. So very, very hard."

CHAPTER 26

Our Fight

A few moments after the Universal Bridge collapsed, leaving a wide swath of emptiness in the sky of the spirit realm, the sphere that had protected Promi and Jaladay dissolved. Yet they hardly noticed. They were embracing each other, aware only of their grief.

Floating together in the mist, they didn't say any words. Nor did they shed any more tears. Their weeping had subsided, leaving them empty of everything but pain. Deep, enduring pain.

Winds swept over them, scattering the shreds of mist. The moaning, shrieking winds sounded like the cries of people who had lost the ones they loved.

At last, Jaladay spoke. "They're gone," she said morosely. "I can't sense their spirits anywhere."

"And they died for no reason," came Promi's bitter reply. "No reason at all—except Narkazan's goals of conquest."

Jaladay pulled herself a small distance away. Taking off her eye band, she peered at her brother. "That's not true, Promi. They died to save *us*. And in that, they succeeded."

Peering into her forest green eyes, Promi gave a slow nod. "They did. But Jaladay . . ." His voice broke.

"Yes," she finished, gently touching his hand. "I, too, would much rather they'd still be alive."

"Still here."

"Yes . . . still here."

"Well now," said a grumpy voice nearby, "that was unexpected."

"Kermi!" Opening her arms, Jaladay gave the monkeylike creature a warm hug. "You found us."

Wrapping his long blue tail around her arm, he said, "That's true. But," he added, staring at the empty space between the bright and dark clusters of worlds, "we seem to have lost the bridge."

Jaladay's eyes moistened again. "We've lost more than that."

Kermi jolted. "You don't mean—"

"Yes," she said despondently. "They're gone! Sammelvar and Escholia are . . ." She paused, struggling to say the word. "Destroyed."

"Terrible, terrible news," said a deep voice above them.

Lifting their heads, they saw Theosor watching them grimly. His invisible wings whirred as he hovered, ruffling his majestic mane.

Shaking his immense head, the wind lion said, "Never again will we know spirits of their wisdom and grace."

"Or courage," added Promi, gazing sadly at his old friend. "They sacrificed their lives to save ours."

Clenching his jaw, he looked from Theosor to Jaladay and back again. "Which is why we must *finish their work*."

"Right," agreed Jaladay. "We must defeat Narkazan."

Promi nodded decisively. "Once and for all."

"True, young cubs." Theosor flew closer. "And we have no time to waste. My scouts have confirmed that he is massing a huge army in the Xarnagg region. He may have gathered all his forces there."

"Except," said Jaladay bitterly, "for the ones who were hiding down in the darkness of Noverro, waiting to ambush us."

Promi sent her an understanding glance. Then, turning back to Theosor, he asked, "Where exactly is Xarnagg?"

"Far past the Caverns of Doom," answered the wind lion. "Evidently, when you stole his original battle plans, he realized that his only chance to succeed was to mass his forces far enough away that we wouldn't learn about it until too late."

Promi nodded. "But your scouts still managed to find out."

"Not without cost," replied Theosor, his rumbling voice dropping even lower than usual. "One of my best lieutenants, the wind lion Hassero, gave his life so we could get this information. When he and his partner were returning with their news, they were attacked—and he threw himself in the path of a flashbolt so his partner could survive."

Gravely, Jaladay and Promi traded glances.

"If we leave right away," Theosor added, "we will still have the advantage of surprise. I have told our forces to wait in hiding for my return."

"We have one more advantage," observed Promi.

"What is that?" asked the wind lion.

"We have the Starstone." Promi tapped his tunic pocket. "In here."

Theosor shook his great mane. "It is good you found it, brave cub. But only because now it's not in the hands of Narkazan. We can never use it as a weapon against him."

"But he was going to use it as a weapon against us, wasn't he?"

"Yes. But only after he corrupted it, reversing its powers. The true Starstone can only be used to magnify *positive* magic—to create, not to destroy."

Disappointed, Promi said, "I see. So we'll just have to defeat Narkazan the old fashioned way."

"Right," agreed Theosor.

Putting her eye band back on, Jaladay asked, "Did Hassero and his partner learn anything else about Narkazan's plans?"

"Nothing. All we know is that, instead of assembling at the Caverns as he originally planned, his army is out at Xarnagg." Theosor's nostrils flared, "But that alone is significant—enough for us to mount a surprise attack."

"Let's go, then, while we still have that option," said Promi. Turning to his sister, he added, "I'll miss you."

"No you won't," she declared.

Puzzled, he peered at her. "What do you mean?"

"I mean, you dolt, that I'm coming with you."

Kermi smirked, and a pair of bubbles leaked from the corner of his mouth. "I love it when you put this manfool in his place."

Ignoring the kermuncle, Promi pressed Jaladay, "Are you sure?"

"As sure as you are," she told him. "This is our fight. For our world." Quietly, she added, "And our parents."

"You're right," her brother agreed. Glancing up at Theosor, he asked, "Can you carry both of us?"

"Absolutely, young cub." The wind lion bobbed his massive head and moved right beside them. "Climb on."

Just before they did, both Jaladay and Promi looked one last time at the twin galaxies Evarra and Noverro. One radiated constant bursts of light and color, while the other swirled in layers upon layers of darkness. Where they had been bound together for many ages, they now existed utterly apart. For now there was no bridge to connect them.

CHAPTER 27

Faith

Flying faster than any wind in the spirit realm, Theosor carried his passengers with both grace and speed. Promi and Jaladay, seated on the lionsteed's back, and Kermi, who had wrapped himself securely around Jaladay's neck, could easily imagine that their bodies had merged with Theosor's. They felt the depth of his breathing, the span of his legs, and the constant vibration of his wings as they vaulted through the shifting mists.

Watching the movement of Theosor's muscular shoulders, Promi understood as never before the sheer power of the wind lion. The great creature's fur gleamed like silver moonlight, while his mane rippled constantly in the wind. And Promi remembered when he'd ridden on this same broad back when they outraced Narkazan and cast the evil spirit into the Maelstrom.

Difficult as that was, young cub, said Theosor, speaking directly into Promi's mind, *this will be much harder. We will not easily defeat Narkazan and his entire army.*

I know, the young man replied. *But defeat them we will.*

Theosor roared, charging through the ever-shifting landscape. On all sides, mountains of mist bloomed out of wispy plains, only to transform into billowy canyons or silvery seas. Constantly evolving, ever remaking itself—this was the spirit realm.

Vaulting into an especially large, shadowy cloud, Theosor abruptly slowed down. Then his passengers suddenly noticed subtle movement all around. Creatures!

In the shadows were dozens of wind lions, scores of people in human form, as well as an array of wide-winged birds, a host of wyverns, a band of huge brown bears, a swarm of bees, and one being who resembled a giant octopus with enormous eyes. And more creatures moved in the more distant mists.

Promi and Jaladay saw immediately that this army had been practicing battle maneuvers. The wind lions were soaring together in bands of five, stopping in unison, then flying faster than before. The bears, though immense, were leaping over one another and dodging blows with great agility. The human warriors were swinging their long silver swords, honing their thrusts and counterthrusts. Meanwhile, the wyverns, who resembled small blue dragons with daggerlike talons, whirled and dived through the mists of the cloud. Not far away, the swarm of bees zipped up and down in tight formation, reversing course instantly on signals only they perceived.

"All cease," rumbled Theosor.

Right away, the warriors stopped practicing and drew closer to their leader. To Promi and Jaladay's surprise, the army was even bigger than they had realized.

"With an army like this," said Promi, "we really do have a chance to defeat Narkazan."

"A good chance," added Jaladay.

Theosor nodded to one particular wind lion, who glided forward. Her coat shone silvery blue, with the extra sparkle of dew from this moist cloud. Although she lacked a mane, she stood just as large as her leader. When she spoke, her voice conveyed both strength and intelligence.

"Yes, Theosor?"

"Shellina, I want to ask you—"

"I would be delighted," finished Shellina. "It would be a pleasure to carry one of your passengers."

Theosor gave a deep-throated chuckle. "You are always one wingbeat ahead of me."

Glancing over his shoulder at Jaladay, Promi said, "I know the feeling."

His sister grinned. Then she turned back to the silvery blue wind lion, her expression more serious. "I am Jaladay, and I'd be most grateful if you would carry me. As well as my friend here, Kermi."

By the way of introduction, Kermi uncoiled himself just enough to blow a small stream of bubbles.

"An honor to meet you both," said the lioness.

"The honor is ours," replied Jaladay. She paused, regarding Shellina through her eye band. "Especially because I sense that you were the partner of the brave lion Hassero, who gave his life to save yours."

Shellina bowed her head slightly, then said, "You are right. He was also . . . my brother."

Frowning, Jaladay replied, "Then I am doubly sorry for your loss." With a deep sigh, she added, "We both know what it's like to lose family."

Padding closer, Shellina's rich brown eyes gazed at Jaladay. "Yes, we do." Nudging Jaladay's leg with her nose, she said, "And we will know much more about each other before this battle is through."

"That's certain." Leaning closer to Theosor's head, Jaladay ran a hand through his mane and whispered, "Thank you, great friend."

"Any time, my dear cub."

Quickly, Jaladay moved over to Shellina. Meanwhile, the lioness traded final thoughts with Theosor about their battle plan. At last, Theosor gave a powerful roar and spoke to the whole group.

"It is time," he declared with a shake of his mane, "to defend the freedoms of this realm!"

A thunderous chorus rose from all sides. It was as if a sudden storm had erupted inside the cloud.

"Our strategy remains unchanged," the wind lion continued. "We will have the advantage of surprise. As well as something even more important—our eternal devotion to each other and this realm."

He shook his great mane. "So from each of you, I expect only this: Your courage. Your loyalty. And your love for all we hold dear."

Another thunderous roar erupted.

As the cheers died down, Theosor said just to Promi, "And from you, brave cub, I expect only the qualities you have shown before. Not long ago, you saved both our lives, as well as the Starstone—and I believe you will now do the same for this realm."

Promi nodded, feeling the wind lion's faith flowing through him. At the same time, he felt a prickling of doubt—the same doubt he'd always felt when others believed in him. Whether it was Atlanta, or his parents, or Jaladay . . . he still wasn't quite sure why they had such faith in him. Even the two friends he'd lost in battle, the kind old monk, Bonlo, and the brave turquoise dragon, Ula-noma, seemed to see more in Promi than he saw in himself.

He drew a deep breath. "You have great faith in me, Theosor. And today . . . I hope to earn it."

"Now we go," bellowed the wind lion. "To Xarnagg—and to victory!"

Out of the cloud they poured, like a great flock of birds (although, in this case, birds comprised only a small portion of the flock). With Theosor in the lead, they flew close together. Yet that formation couldn't disguise their great diversity. For they really had only one quality in common: their vows to protect the spirit realm from domination by Narkazan.

Riding on Theosor's back, Promi watched their surroundings change rapidly. They flew through misty canyons and over pinnacles that grew taller by the second. They plunged into a swirling tunnel of colored winds, a place where a gust of bright yellow blew into a cyclone of deep blue that was suddenly swept aside by a gale of orange and green. And they soared past a world of wondrous sounds, where stringlike clouds vibrated constantly, misty flutes blew haunting notes, and vaporous drums pounded echoing rhythms.

Onward they flew. All Promi knew about their route was that they would fly past the Caverns of Doom, not far from Narkazan's old lair in the icicle cloud where Promi had rescued Jaladay. After the Caverns, they would pass near Arcna Ruel, the cloud castle built by Narkazan before he'd been toppled—though that defeat had turned out to be only temporary. Somewhere in the misty lands beyond Arcna Ruel, Promi knew, lay the little-explored region of Xarnagg.

Theosor, who had been listening to Promi's thoughts, spoke again into his mind. *You remember that cloud castle well, don't you, bold cub? It was there you first found the Starstone—and Narkazan.*

Promi nodded, his long locks streaming behind as they flew. *I'll never forget it.*

Nor will I, as long as my mane keeps growing. Theosor added, *In fact, Narkazan was recently spotted back at Arcna Ruel. That makes sense, since his army is gathering not far beyond there.*

The wind lion abruptly turned and dived straight into a watery cloud as dense as a lake. For a few seconds, they were submerged completely in cold water, unable to breathe. Then, just as abruptly, they burst out of the cloud, trailing a silvery stream of mist.

Glancing to the rear, Promi saw that all the warriors were still flying right behind them in close formation. While they now looked wetter than when he'd first seen them, their expressions made it clear that they were still every bit as determined to prevail. And to end Narkazan's ambitions once and for all.

Looking closely at Jaladay, who was leaning forward with her arms wrapped around Shellina's sturdy neck, Promi felt a surge of pride. *She is made of strong stuff, that sister of mine. After all she's been through—she's now riding into battle.*

Then, in his head, he heard a voice—Jaladay's voice. *The same could be said for you, brother of mine.*

Promi grinned. He turned forward again, and almost immediately noticed a drop in temperature. Soon it grew cold enough that he could see Theosor's breath, blowing white clouds from the lion's nostrils as the wings continued to whir. Before long, Promi started to see ice crystals floating all around—some of them as small and slender as a finger, others as massive as a mountain.

Just ahead appeared a massive gray cloud whose entire surface was pocked with lightless pits. The Caverns of Doom.

Passing the abandoned caverns, Promi shivered—not just from

the cold. He felt a wave of relief that at least their battle wouldn't be fought at that ominous place.

Boom! A powerful blast suddenly exploded out of one of the caverns!

Careening sharply, Theosor swerved just an instant before a flashbolt, burning with intense white flame, zipped right in front of his nose. Half a second later, the flashbolt would have surely hit the wind lion, as well as Promi.

"Attack!" roared Theosor. "We're under attack!"

CHAPTER 28

Battle for the Spirit Realm

Like deadly missiles, Narkazan's forces poured out of the Caverns of Doom. Because each dark pit was, in fact, a sizeable chamber, out of each flew large groups of warriors—including hundreds and hundreds of mistwraiths.

Caught completely unprepared, the band of defenders lost their tight formation. Theosor swerved so sharply that Promi clung with all his strength to the lion's mane. An instant later, Theosor came around to lead a charge at the oncoming forces.

"Stay light, stay nimble!" roared the wind lion. "Avoid mistwraiths and attack the rest!"

Promi saw instantly that they were greatly outnumbered. In addition to the mistwraiths, who quickly formed bands of ten or twelve to converge on individual foes, came a horde of immortals of many varieties. Some took human form, archers with deadly black arrows and powerful bows, wearing uniforms of creamy satin robes. With them flew at least half a dozen red-winged dragons, a whole phalanx of insect-like beasts with twisting tongues, and a band of huge lizards with jagged wings and jaws full of sword-sharp teeth.

Strangest of all came a line of liquid beasts. They flowed through the air, jaws wide open, teeth bubbling in their watery mouths. Shrieking with high, ear-splitting voices, the liquid beasts were wrath in fluid form.

Yet as fierce as those warriors were, none were more terrifying than the mistwraiths. Like shadowy comets, they left trails of darkness in their wakes. Crackling with deadly sparks, they bore down on the defenders, determined to spare no wind lions or eagles or people.

Narkazan, for his part, flew at the rear of this horde. Unlike Theosor, who led the defenders' charge, the attackers' leader seemed content to let his troops do most of the fighting. Yet he kept a sharp eye on Theosor—as well as his passenger, the young man who bore the mark of the Prophecy.

At this moment, that mark on Promi's chest was burning with anxious heat. *Shouldn't I fly separately?* he asked the wind lion urgently. *So you can maneuver better?*

Not yet, young cub. Right now you should stay with me.

Another flashbolt shot out of the caverns. Again, Theosor turned abruptly and barely dodged it. The flashbolt crashed into an enormous floating ice crystal that exploded into millions of frozen shards.

Ducking his head as shards flew over them, Promi said to the wind lion, *I see your point.*

Tightening his hold on the shaggy mane, Promi glanced back

at Jaladay, hugging the neck of the lioness Shellina. The bold defender suddenly changed course, flying straight through a band of archers. Her deft move cost several archers their weapons, which snapped or went hurtling, and broke the bones of several others. The band, now scattered, was no more use to Narkazan.

Just then, Theosor leaped straight up—and plowed right into two of the red dragons who had been soaring into battle. Using his head as a battering ram, the wind lion broke the ribs of one dragon, who shrieked in pain, then smashed through the outstretched wing of the other. That dragon spun out of control and crashed into a block of ice the size of a huge boulder.

Theosor immediately veered to the left, so suddenly that Promi almost fell off the wind lion's back. He regained his balance just as Theosor made a most dangerous maneuver. Seconds before a large group of mistwraiths closed in on a trio of wind lions, Theosor flew right through the middle of the attackers, roaring angrily.

Promi closed his eyes as they plunged through the mass of shadowy beings. For an instant that seemed more like an hour, the entire world went utterly dark. He felt weak, unable to draw even a single breath. At the same time, black sparks crackled all around—and despite the cold temperature, Promi felt suddenly so hot he could burn to ashes.

All at once, they burst out of the thick folds of blackness that had surrounded them. The intense heat vanished, except for the continued burning Promi felt on his chest. Suddenly he noticed a black spark that had landed on Theosor's mane, sizzling dangerously. Before it could do any damage, Promi drew his dagger and used the blade to sweep the spark aside.

As he replaced the dagger, Promi glanced behind. The mistwraiths Theosor had charged were reeling in surprise, crackling angrily as they spun in circles, totally disoriented. And they had lost their opportunity to attack those wind lions.

Other defenders, however, weren't so fortunate. One massive eagle, swarmed by mistwraiths, screeched in agony. As the dark cloud of attackers closed around the bird, the screeching abruptly stopped. When the mistwraiths parted, only a single feather remained, twirling slowly downward.

Many more defenders met the same fate, including several wind lions. Even the big-eyed octopus, whose girth was wider than a band of mistwraiths, shrieked in terror as a group surrounded him. He managed to escape by whirling his many appendages, confusing the attackers, but he then flew right into the line of liquid beasts. Gurgling furiously, the beasts coalesced around the octopus.

Before Promi could see what happened next, Theosor swerved to avoid a gigantic ice crystal. The pack of winged lizards who had been tailing them closely had no time to react—and smashed headlong into the mass of ice.

"Look out!" cried Jaladay, riding Shellina just above them.

Both wind lions veered sharply, barely avoiding a volley of black arrows. It took all the strength in Promi's arms and legs to hold on. Glancing over at his sister, he felt relieved to see that she, too, had clung to her lionsteed.

Boom! A flashbolt flew past, white-hot, so close that Promi and Jaladay, as well as their wind lions, felt the burst of intense heat. It struck a man and woman who had just evaded a pack of mistwraiths. Their bodies ignited, sizzled, and then vanished completely.

Promi and Jaladay both winced. Such a vivid reminder of how painfully—and recently—their parents had died!

All around, the battle raged. Two defenders, wielding silver swords, fought desperately against a frenzied flock of insect beasts whose long tongues slashed like whips. When one of the beasts wrapped its tongue around a swordfighter's arm and moved closer to devour its prey—the other swordfighter swung her blade and severed the tongue completely.

Meanwhile, three burly bears dared to pounce on top of a huge red dragon. Roaring wildly, they rode precariously on their foe (two on its back and one on its wing) while it tried to shake them loose. As the dragon spun in tight circles, shrieking angrily and slashing with its talons, the bears tore at its scales with teeth and claws.

As a mass of mistwraiths surrounded a wind lion, closing in for the kill, a swarm of bees and a blue wyvern tore into the attackers. They managed to distract the mistwraiths long enough for the lion to escape . . . but the wyvern and most of the bees perished in the rescue.

Just then, at the edge of his vision, Promi saw something that made his blood boil with fury. Riding on the back of one red dragon was a satin-robed man with a pallid face and dark, vengeful eyes. Grukarr!

Promi glared at the wicked priest who had tried to kill Atlanta—as well as Promi, several times over. Who had masterminded Narkazan's earlier attempt to conquer all the mortal creatures on Earth. Who had tried to impose the True Religion, as he called it, on the people of Atlantis. And who had, most recently, caused the terrible death of the loyal monk, Bonlo.

Gritting his teeth, Promi sent Theosor a new thought. *Time to part, old friend! I have some work to do.*

Even as Theosor roared in disapproval, Promi flew off the wind lion's back. Dodging a cloud of crackling mistwraiths, he shot straight at his old enemy. Judging his angle carefully, he aimed himself like a human missile, both fists held in front of him.

A heartbeat later, Grukarr looked around. Suddenly seeing Promi bearing down on him, the evil priest opened his mouth wide to scream in fright. But he had no time to make any sound.

Slam! Promi crashed into Grukarr's neck, knocking him completely off his perch on the dragon's back. Wailing in pain, clutching his neck, Grukarr spun downward.

The dragon, by contrast, wasn't so easy to deal with. The enormous beast roared, enraged—then whirled around and swatted Promi full force with its bony, batlike wing. Reeling in pain, Promi realized that he'd failed to think about what would happen *after* striking Grukarr—a mistake that an experienced warrior like Theosor would never have made.

His head spinning from the blow, Promi saw the angry dragon swing around, deadly talons raised to tear him to shreds. Meanwhile, eyes shining like incandescent rubies glowered at this little man who had dared to attack a warrior dragon.

The huge beast snarled, opening its jaws to the widest to swallow Promi once its talons impaled him. Desperately, Promi looked around for any sources of help. But Theosor was deep in battle with a swarm of insect beasts. And Shellina was nowhere in sight.

Baring hundreds of bloodstained teeth, the red dragon roared. Its talons started to slice through the air, ready to rip into its helpless prey.

Forgive me! Promi called to everyone he'd ever loved, certain those would be his very last words.

The talons, gleaming with the light of another flashbolt, sliced toward him at lightning speed. Just before they tore into Promi—

Thud!

Something slammed into the dragon, knocking it backward so hard that it flipped over completely. Its talons ripped through the air by Promi's face, missing him by a hair, as the dragon roared with unbridled fury.

Then another roar erupted. It came from whatever creature had arrived in time to save Promi. And he knew instantly that this, too, was the roar of a powerful dragon. A dragon he knew well.

"Ulanoma!" he cried, astonished, as well as grateful, to see his old friend. "You're alive!"

The turquoise dragon, taller but more slender than the one who'd been just about to tear Promi apart, shot him a glance from her diamond-shaped eyes. "So arrrrre you, Prrrrrometheus," she boomed. "But only just barrrrrely."

"Thanks to you," he replied.

"And don't forget your other old friend," called a much smaller voice. It came from an old, white-haired monk who was riding atop the turquoise dragon's brow, clinging to the starfish that had attached to the dragon's scales like undersea jewelry.

"Bonlo—Bonlo, it's you!"

"Aye, it is, good lad." The monk gave him a wink. "You don't think a little swim in the sea would be enough to end my story, do you?"

Promi shook his head in disbelief. "I was sure you'd drowned."

"So was I, lad, until this loyal dragon-friend hauled me out of the deep abyss and revived me with her magical breath."

Ulanoma nodded, swaying the huge chunk of ocean glass that hung from one of her ears, held by a net of mermaids' hair. "Afterrrrr I evaded those mistwrrrrraiths wherrrrre we parrrrrted, I went back to the sea to searrrrrch forrrrr yourrrrr frrrrriend."

"For which," added Bonlo with a pat on her massive brow, "I'm most grateful."

The turquoise dragon's eyes narrowed with worry. She waved a wing at the battle raging all around them, and her ocean-glass earring instantly darkened. "Now herrrrre we arrrrre again, surrrr-rounded by mistwrrrrraiths."

Promi scanned their surroundings. Immediately, his heart sank. Mistwraiths swarmed everywhere. At least half of the spirit realm's defenders had been lost. And the brave warriors loyal to Theosor who remained were all fighting for their lives, vastly outnumbered.

On top of all that, Narkazan's forces kept blasting away with the most deadly weapon of all—the flashbolt cannon. Every time it fired one of its supercharged blasts, more defenders perished. A few more strikes . . . and Theosor's forces would be decimated.

"Keep fighting, you two!" Promi called to his brave friends the sea dragon and the monk. "There's something I need to do."

Instantly, he flew off—straight for the cavern holding the flash-bolt cannon. Seeing this, Ulanoma roared in protest. "You can't do that alone, Prrrrrometheus! You will—"

Her shout ended abruptly when the huge red dragon returned, smashing into her back with devastating force. Ulanoma roared in pain, as well as rage. Regaining her balance, she wheeled around and used her wing to scoop up Bonlo, who had been knocked completely off his perch. Tossing him back atop her brow, the tur-quoise dragon plunged into battle with her foe. Eyes ablaze, the two enormous warriors tore into each other using their tails, wings, and talons, along with their immense bodies.

Meanwhile, Promi sped away on a mission of his own.

CHAPTER 29

The Flashbolt Cannon

While the battle roiled the sky, Promi zoomed straight toward one particular cavern in the massive gray cloud where Narkazan's forces had launched their attack. From that cavern, he'd seen several blasts from the flashbolt cannon—blasts that had been utterly devastating to the defenders of the spirit realm.

Not bothering to veer aside to disguise his route, he flew like a human arrow at the cavern. *My only chance,* he told himself, *is speed. To get there before they fire another blast!*

A heartbeat later, light all around him dimmed as he entered the thick mist of the cloud. Straight ahead, he could see the mouth of the tunnel. Deep within it, he glimpsed a powerful new light starting to swell in strength—the next flash-bolt, getting ready to fire!

Promi shifted course slightly to aim not directly at the flash-bolt—which would have sent him right into the cannon—but at the huge warrior who was sitting at the rear of the cannon, working its controls. A warrior whose immense hulk, angry scowl, and four muscular arms he recognized from his first trip to the spirit realm. A warrior whose brutal kind he'd hoped never to meet again.

An amber giant.

In that final instant before he struck, Promi saw that this amber giant was even bigger than the ones he'd fought before. Seated at the cannon's controls, the massive warrior's four arms were rapidly adjusting levers to prepare for the next blast. The whole cannon, made of ultrahardened vaporstone, was vibrating with energy, making a loud whirring sound that grew steadily louder. At the same time, the light inside the cannon's muzzle grew brighter.

Slam! Promi plowed full force into the giant.

The huge warrior flew backward into the cavern, smashing into a wall of ice. He hit so hard that ice shards exploded everywhere and the entire wall collapsed, burying the warrior.

Promi, who had rammed into the giant with his shoulder, rolled on the cavern floor. Momentarily dazed from the impact, he shook himself and sat up. Rubbing his sore shoulder, he realized what had happened to the giant.

A rush of satisfaction surged through him. *Success! Now I need to turn off that cursed cannon—and find some way to put it out of action!*

He stood up, approaching the controls even as the cannon's vibrations rose to deafening levels. Inside the muzzle, the flashbolt swelled to maximum brightness.

Hurriedly, he tried to make sense of the controls. More than a dozen levers were engaged—which is why it helped to have four arms to operate them. *But which one,* he asked himself, mind racing, *will stop this thing?*

Suddenly he noticed, at the edge of the control panel, two large buttons—one red, one black. Guessing that the black one would shut down the cannon, he lunged for it. Just as his finger was about to reach it—

The collapsed wall of ice exploded! With a roar of rage even louder than the cannon's vibrations, the amber giant burst out from under the debris and shoved Promi aside with brutal force. The young man flew into the opposite wall, striking so hard that he fell to the floor, his mind spinning.

Before he could get up, the amber-skinned warrior grabbed him by the throat and lifted him up high. Bellowing wrathfully, the giant's massive hand squeezed hard, choking the life out of this intruder. Losing consciousness fast, Promi did the only thing he could—he kicked with all his might.

But he missed completely. With all his remaining strength, even as darkness fell over his thoughts, he tried again.

That kick connected with the giant's throat. The warrior grunted in pain and fell backward, dropping Promi on the cavern floor.

Forcing himself to stand, Promi scanned his surroundings for some way to fight this four-armed behemoth. By now, the giant had recovered and was starting to charge. At the same time, the cannon's vibrations shook the whole cavern, so vigorously that a row of huge icicles on the ceiling cracked and smashed to the floor.

Promi darted aside just as the giant lunged at him and bashed into the wall. Seizing his chance, Promi rolled under the cannon's muzzle. On the cannon's other side, he bounced to his feet, putting the big weapon between the two of them.

Angered beyond anything in his experience, the amber warrior waved all four arms wildly, even as he bellowed like an erupting volcano. Another row of icicles cracked and plunged down, splintering on top of the cannon.

Taking advantage of this distraction, Promi dashed toward the controls. The instant before he reached the black button, though, the giant threw a chunk of ice that struck Promi hard in the chest. He tumbled backward, slamming into the wall.

Right above him, the biggest icicle in the cavern cracked and wobbled. Seeing this, Promi had an idea—a wild, desperate idea.

As the giant leaped across the cannon and raced toward him, bursting with desire to grab this intruder and rip his body into hundreds of pieces, Promi didn't run. Instead, he used his final split second to leap up and swat the bottom tip of the enormous icicle. He connected—just as the giant barreled into him and sent him flying backward into the wall.

At the same instant Promi hit the wall, the icicle plunged down on top of the giant. Piercing the warrior's muscular shoulder close to his neck, the weighty icicle collapsed right on him. Though he was too strong to be killed, the giant howled in agony and tumbled into the cannon itself. So heavy was his immense body, the force swung the weapon around so that its muzzle no longer faced the mouth of the cavern. Instead, the cannon now pointed at a sidewall.

Shrieking with rage, bleeding profusely from his wound, the giant hurled himself at Promi. But the young man hardly noticed. A new idea flared inside his mind—an idea that might well cost him his own life . . . but could silence forever Narkazan's most deadly weapon.

Promi lunged at the cannon. Reaching out his arm, he slammed a fist on the controls. Instead of hitting the black button, though, he hit the red one.

Instantly, the cannon's vibrations ceased with a loud *snap*. A super intense blast of energy exploded out of the cannon—right into the cavern wall. Huge blocks of ice crashed down as the cavern imploded, shaking the entire cloud.

Ice crystals flew in all directions, creating fog so thick that it covered all the Caverns of Doom. The fog lasted only a few seconds, but just before it cleared, a lone warrior emerged from the swirling mists.

Promi burst out of the vapors. Though his shoulder ached and his eyes stung from the powerful blast, he was still alive. Still in one piece. And still as eager as ever to defeat Narkazan.

Now to finish the job! he told himself triumphantly. Regaining his bearings, he sped off to rejoin the others.

CHAPTER 30

Desperation

As fast as a comet, Promi raced back to his fellow defenders. He couldn't wait to tell them the flashbolt cannon was no longer a threat.

He veered around a huge block of ice and the battle came into view. The instant he saw the defenders, though, his heart sank. They still battled furiously, for sure. But their numbers had diminished markedly from when he'd left on his mission. Clouds of utterly dark mist-wraiths surrounded many of them, while red dragons tore furiously into anyone within reach—whether wind lions or bears, humans or bees.

Straining to see through all the ice crystals floating everywhere, Promi thought he caught a glimpse of Theosor, bravely fighting a pair of red dragons. And he spotted Ulanoma's long neck as she swooped into a mass of mistwraiths, her wings spread wide. Whether or not Bonlo was still with her, Promi couldn't tell. And amidst the fray, he saw no sign of Jaladay or her lionsteed Shellina.

Promi zoomed into the battle, surprising a band of Narkazan's archers who were just about to release a volley at a pair of wind lions. Slamming into them from the side, Promi hit them with all his force. Arrows, bows, and archers tumbled, while the wind lions escaped unharmed.

Just as he spun around, Promi happened to glance back at the huge gray cloud he'd left only moments before. While the cavern that once held the flashbolt cannon had now collapsed completely, what caught his attention was another cavern entirely.

Much larger than the others, the mouth of this cavern was surrounded by a group of mistwraiths. Were they guarding the entrance? If so . . . why?

His answer appeared as an immense vehicle emerged from the entrance. Standing atop it was Narkazan himself, his hands on his hips. The warlord's tusks flashed in the light as he barked orders to a pair of winged ogres who were moving the vehicle into place.

Suddenly, as the contraption swung around, Promi saw a huge vaporstone muzzle that extended from its core. Pointing right in his direction!

A cannon! he realized with a jolt. *Another cannon, even bigger than the first one!*

"Promi!"

Jaladay's shout made him whirl around. He felt a wave of relief that she was still alive, though her robe was torn and she'd lost her eye band. Kermi, too, had suffered, evidenced by the burned fur on his back and tail. Shellina, though, had fared worse: A savage gash ran all the way from her neck to her hindquarters, oozing blood.

At that moment, a proud head covered with turquoise scales emerged from behind a massive cluster of crystals. Ulanoma! And there, riding on her brow, was old Bonlo—still alive, though his monk's robe had been scorched by dragon fire. Swiftly, they flew toward Promi.

Flying erratically to avoid a volley of arrows, Theosor came right behind them. As the great wind lion approached, Promi noticed something new in that proud face crowned with a mane. Something he'd never expected to see.

Desperation.

"Promi," called Jaladay again. "Leave now! The battle is lost."

"Now, young cub!" roared Theosor. "We must escape while we still can! Before he fires the—"

An enormous *boom!* rocked the entire region. Shot from Narkazan's huge cannon, the blast flew swifter than lightning—and slammed directly into Promi and his friends.

CHAPTER 31

The Greatest Single Force

Struck by the blast from Narkazan's cannon, Promi expected to perish instantly—incinerated just as his parents had been. Instead, something very different happened.

An enormous net, shot from the cannon, opened fully just before it hit Promi and his friends. All of them—Promi and Jaladay, Kermi (still clinging to Jaladay's neck), the two wind lions, as well as the turquoise dragon and her passenger Bonlo—were thrown backward by the force. The net, made from fibrous strands of vaporstone, closed around the whole group.

With a terrible crash, they slammed into an immense wall of ice bigger than a hillside. Tiny ice crystals rained down on them from the impact, while the powerful grappling hooks attached to the edges of the net sank deeply into the wall.

Ulanoma roared in rage. The turquoise dragon arched her powerful back and thrashed her long neck, trying with all her might to break out of the net. Theosor and Shellina did the same, swiping at the net with their paws and twisting madly to free themselves. But their motions only drove the hooks deeper into the ice.

Meanwhile, the more they struggled, the tighter the net wrapped around them. All the dragon got for her efforts were dozens of lost scales, pried loose by the net. Even the strength of two great wind lions did nothing to break their bonds.

Seizing his dagger, Promi tried desperately to hack away at the strands. Yet his blade didn't even make a dent on the vaporstone fibers. He kept trying, regardless, even when his arm and back ached from the strain.

"Don't spend yourself," said Jaladay glumly. "This net can't be broken."

Promi scowled, fearing she was right. But before he re-sheathed his dagger, he turned to a different kind of weapon—the skills of a Listener. Focusing on the net, he used that remarkable sense to probe its innermost fibers, trying to hear the secrets of how it had been woven. And how it might possibly be broken.

Deeper and deeper he probed, searching for any sort of weakness. Any flaw at all.

None, he concluded sadly. *This net really is invulnerable.*

"As I told you," said Jaladay, having heard his thoughts. Though her face remained grim, she gave her brother a wan smile. "But you wouldn't be Promi if you didn't try anyway."

He sighed. "What can we do, trapped in a net that's unbreakable?"

"We wait," answered Theosor, his rumbling voice weighed down by despair. "For the inevitable."

"Not so fast," piped up Bonlo. Pinned against one of the dragon's huge ears, he said quietly, "This net may be unbreakable . . . but so is our courage."

Like a faint charge of electricity, the elder monk's words sent a current through everyone. A current of hope. In Ulanoma's ocean-glass earring, the smallest spark of light appeared in the dense darkness.

"Well, well," rasped a harsh voice outside the net. "Isn't this a lovely sight?"

Narkazan peered at them, trapped completely, as he floated just out of reach. Hovering beside him, a pair of mistwraiths crackled vengefully, their dark folds rippling.

Theosor roared mightily, as did Shellina and the turquoise dragon. But Narkazan merely folded his thin arms and scoffed at them. "Is that all the noise you can make? Such a pity."

Ignoring the chorus of angry growls, their tormentor drifted closer, so that his narrow chin almost touched the net's strands. Seeing Jaladay astride a wind lion, he rasped, "How nice to see you again, my jewel, my prize. I knew you would come back to me eventually."

Jaladay shot him a look more piercing than any blade. "I did come back. But only to destroy you!"

The scars on Narkazan's face darkened until they resembled rivers that ran with blood. "You will soon regret your impudence," he said coldly.

Turning to Promi, the warrior spirit taunted, "I was so *very* sorry to hear about your parents' demise. What a great shame! Imagine losing all those eons of wisdom in one fiery instant."

So much raw emotion flooded Promi that it clogged his mind,

as well as his throat. He just stared, speechless, at Narkazan. So did Jaladay.

Cackling softly, their captor continued, "I speak truthfully. I *was* disappointed that they died in that flashbolt." Lowering his voice, he added, "Much too quickly! I would have delighted in finding ways to *prolong* their misery."

"If anyone deserves prolonged misery," said Promi hoarsely, "it's you."

Narkazan stroked the tip of his pointed chin. "Fear not, son of the Prophecy. I shall not make that same mistake with you! Or your sister the Seer. Or," he added with a nod at the other prisoners, "with any of your ragtag allies."

Behind him, the mistwraiths crackled approvingly, releasing a shower of black sparks. One of those sparks landed on the net, sizzling on a strand. Glancing down, Promi watched it, hoping it might burn through the fiber. Alas, the spark fell away, leaving nothing more than a charred smudge.

Still gazing at Promi, Narkazan added casually, "That also goes, by the way, for any allies you have on Earth."

Seeing Promi tense, the warlord clucked with satisfaction. "Or have you not yet heard about my little gift to your old world?"

"I've heard about that bloodthirsty monster you set loose, if that's what you mean."

"Quite so," answered Narkazan. "But my guess is you don't yet comprehend its full purpose. While the wretched beast *thinks* it exists to eat and eat some more . . . its real purpose is much more subtle."

"You mean more murderous," retorted Promi, wriggling under the net.

"You're on the right track, son of the Prophecy. That monster will devour any mortals who might ever be tempted to oppose my invasion of Atlantis—all before I even arrive on the island."

"Coward!" spat Promi. "You're nothing but a coward!"

Ignoring him, Narkazan calmly stroked his chin. "Ah, but the *best* thing about my monster is not what it will do to the people on Atlantis. No . . . its supreme accomplishment will be what it does to all the rest of the people on Earth."

"What? You mean—"

"No need for me to explain. Certainly not to *you*. But you can take my word that the monster carries something quite powerful. Something that will swiftly destroy any mortal foes I might ever have to meet. All before I meet them, of course."

Before Promi could ask any questions, Narkazan rasped, "But enough about the future! Let's talk about the present—by which I mean the various tortures that await you."

The warlord paused, allowing his threat to sink in. "I have such wondrous tortures in mind for you, son of the Prophecy."

When Promi set his jaw defiantly, Narkazan added, "As well as your sister and your friends." Lowering his voice, he said, "But most of all, your sister."

Seeing Promi wince, he crowed, "Such glorious agonies await you all!" Tapping one of his tusks thoughtfully, he added, "Unless . . ."

"Unless what?"

Peering at the captive young man, Narkazan said, "I would be willing to change my plans on one condition."

Doubtful, Promi raised an eyebrow.

The warlord's stern expression hardened even more. "I cannot possibly resist torturing you, Promi, in the most painful ways ever devised. I have relished that prospect far too long to abandon it now."

He shook his head, making his earring hit repeatedly against one of his tusks. "However, I *would* promise to spare the life of your sister, Jaladay . . . if you accept my condition."

Cautiously, Promi asked, "What do you want?"

Narkazan replied with a single phrase: "The Starstone."

Promi caught his breath. "You know I have it?"

"Yes. I can sense its presence, its power, even now." Narkazan frowned. "With the tortures I have planned for you, the precious crystal could be damaged. Compromised. But if you give it to me of your own volition . . . the Starstone would be spared. And so would your sister."

"Don't do it!" shouted Jaladay. "I would much rather die than have the crystal in his evil hands."

Narkazan gave her a sharp look. "You may say that now, my jewel. Yet when you encounter my most excruciating treatments, you will change your mind. Oh yes, you certainly will."

"Never," she vowed.

Promi gazed at her—his sister, his only sibling, his great friend. If he actually *could* somehow save her life . . . wouldn't that be worth something? Maybe even something as precious as the Starstone?

His face twisted with uncertainty. He had done so much wrong in his brief life! He'd failed to tell Atlanta what he truly felt for her, just as he'd failed to protect Atlantis. And that very day, he'd failed to save the lives of Sammelvar and Escholia—his own parents, as well as the beloved leaders of their people.

Feeling the bulge in his tunic pocket, he wondered, *Is this my last chance to do at least one thing right?*

Promi's mind whirled. Doubts, questions, and ideas all wrestled with each other, circling and circling, faster and faster.

"No more delaying, son of the Prophecy." Narkazan's harsh voice pierced his thoughts like a dagger. "What is your decision?"

All at once, in that instant, Promi knew exactly what he must do.

Twisting under the net, he created just enough room to reach his hand into his pocket. With a dismal sigh, he pulled out the Starstone.

"No!" cried Jaladay.

"Don't do it, young cub," rumbled Theosor.

Yet Promi didn't seem to hear. Though he still held the Starstone inside the net, he started to slowly reach through the webbing toward the warlord.

Extending his own hand, Narkazan grinned eagerly, the expression of a hungry man about to taste his most favorite food.

"Please, Promi," cried Jaladay. "Don't do this!"

"Resist, young cub. Resist!"

The mistwraiths crackled louder than ever, quaking with excitement.

Promi, however, wasn't listening. Instead, he was hearing other voices—voices from the past.

The veil, announced Sammelvar sadly, *is destroyed. Gone forever.* His face grim, he continued, *All that magical energy—once the greatest single force in the spirit realm—is now lost, scattered everywhere.*

Again and again, Promi heard those phrases in his memory.

All that magical energy.

The greatest single force in the spirit realm.

Scattered everywhere.

At the same time, he heard another voice from memory: Theosor's clear warning about the Starstone.

We can never use it as a weapon, young cub. The Starstone can only be used to magnify positive magic—to create, not to destroy.

Those phrases, too, echoed in his mind.

Never use it as a weapon.

Only to magnify positive magic.

To create, not destroy.

Sammelvar spoke again, his voice rich with both wisdom and love. *All that magical energy.*

And Theosor roared his reply. *Create—not destroy.*

Squeezing the Starstone in his hand, Promi turned his full attention to the present. Silently calling to the magical crystal, he pleaded, *Hear me, Starstone. Grant me one last wish—one last creation.*

He poured all his energy into conveying that wish. So hard did he squeeze the crystal, his hand shook with pain.

Narkazan, watching carefully, thought Promi was shaking with fear and doubt. In his most silky voice, he coaxed, "Come now, Promi. Hand it to me."

Reaching his bony hand closer to the net, the warlord urged, "That's right. You keep your part of the bargain and I'll keep mine."

Promi reached through the net. He started to open his hand— just enough that a single facet of the crystal brushed against Narkazan's fingertip.

Instantly, the Starstone flashed with all the brilliance of a new-born star. Narkazan reeled, crying out and covering his eyes. Behind him, the mistwraiths screeched angrily.

In that instant, Promi's wish—a wish with two parts—came true.

First, from every corner of the realm, all the old magic of the veil rekindled. Instead of scattering aimlessly, all that energy— amounting to the most powerful force in the spirit realm— instantly reversed course and coalesced in a single, concentrated sphere that completely enveloped Narkazan. As well as the pair of mistwraiths. Squeezing down on them like an impenetrable bubble, the newly constituted sphere created a transparent shield around the realm's greatest enemy—a shield that would contain him for all time.

"Let me out!" shrieked Narkazan as he pounded on the sphere. Though the container muffled his exact words, his meaning could not have been more clear.

Enraged beyond any description, his eyes flashed and his skin turned purple. Wrathfully, he kicked at the mistwraiths unlucky enough to be trapped inside the sphere with him. But all his violent kicking accomplished was to jostle the sphere, making its captives even more uncomfortable.

Pressing his face against the sphere, Narkazan's gaze met Promi's. While the warlord continued to rant, however, all Promi did was grin. For both of them knew that Narkazan would be confined in that prison for eternity.

The moment Narkazan's warriors realized that their leader had been captured, they abruptly ceased fighting. For they knew that, without their leader, they were destined for certain defeat. As if on command, all the mistwraiths, red dragons, insect beasts, and others either surrendered or fled into hiding. Soon all that remained of Narkazan's army was the sphere, floating aimlessly on whatever breeze might touch it.

The second part of Promi's wish happened in that same remarkable moment: The vaporstone net dissolved! Suddenly, Promi and his companions were all free.

Jaladay leaped off Shellina's back and hugged her brother. Gazing at him—or, it seemed to Promi, through him—she said amidst her laughter and tears, "For my thick-headed brother, you can be very clever sometimes."

"Thanks," he replied. "Maybe I learned a few things from you."

"Just a few," she agreed. Then she hugged him again.

"And I must add," said Kermi crustily, "you can blow a pretty fair bubble."

Promi smiled, knowing that he'd just heard the nicest remark that Kermi would ever say to him.

Theosor's muzzle nudged the young man. He gave his wild mane a vigorous shake, as if freeing himself completely from confinement. His voice rumbling like thunder, he declared, "You did well, brave cub. Your parents would be proud."

Running his hand through the silvery mane, Promi nodded. "Thank you, my friend."

Feeling a gentle tap on his shoulder, he turned to see Bonlo. A wide grin creased the monk's face. "There is something you should know, good lad."

"What's that?"

The old fellow scratched his white head, then replied, "When I write the revised history of the spirit and mortal realms, I plan to feature prominently one young man who had a certain, well, *greatness* about him. That was clear, even in that miserable dungeon where we first met."

"Be sure to say," Promi told him, "that the young man would have been completely worthless without his mentors. Especially one old monk who always believed in him, even when he didn't believe in himself."

Bonlo's grin widened even more.

Suddenly Theosor roared. "Promi! I just heard a message for you—an urgent message from the mortal realm."

"What is it? Who sent it?"

The wind lion pawed at the air. "It came from your friend Shangri. She says you must come quickly! Atlanta . . ."

"Tell me!"

Theosor growled before he spoke again. "Atlanta is dying."

CHAPTER 32

Time to Die

Faster than any wind that ever roared across the spirit realm, Theosor carried Promi back to Atlantis. For the young man, even feeling the bulge of the Starstone, safely in his pocket again, wasn't enough to turn his thoughts back to the surprising defeat of Narkazan. Or the unanswered question of how Narkazan's monster could destroy everyone on Earth. No, all Promi's thoughts—and all his passions—were now focused on Atlanta.

Dying! he told himself, feeling the bite of that word like a whip striking his back. *Shangri said she's dying!*

As they burst through the clouds above the mortal world and approached the island that he himself had created, Promi wondered where on Atlantis he should look for her. Time was clearly of the essence—every second mattered.

Suddenly, as they plunged nearer, he saw towering plumes of smoke rising from the City of Great Powers. And if he wasn't mistaken, the largest and blackest plume of all originated at the Divine Monk's temple.

"Take me there," he called to Theosor, pointing at the billowing cloud above the temple.

"As you wish, brave cub," the wind lion rumbled.

A few seconds later, Theosor touched down on a deserted street across from the ruins of the temple. Promi hopped off, his bare feet slapping the stones—then hurriedly turned to his old friend. They shared an instantaneous look—and while no words were spoken, the look itself said everything.

Promi turned away. Behind him, he heard a sudden gust of wind. On that wind came a familiar roar that lingered for a moment . . . and then vanished.

Facing the temple grounds, he immediately saw that the entry gates had been destroyed. Beyond, the Divine Monk's residence was now nothing but a pile of burning rubble, as were most of the other buildings. Even the bell tower had collapsed; the bell itself lay broken and forever silent.

Where in this mess am I going to find her? he thought frantically.

Suddenly he knew what to do. Drawing on his abilities as a Listener, he concentrated on Atlanta. Her heartbeat. Her vitality and love of life that flowed through every vein and artery.

But he couldn't hear her. *Atlanta . . . where are you?*

Reaching out with his hearing, he searched for the sound of her heart. He kneeled down in the street, pushing aside all the other sounds that swirled everywhere. With all his determination, he focused entirely on the one person, the one heart, he so desperately wanted to find.

Success! Promi stood up, hearing Atlanta's heartbeat at last. Yet . . . it was very faint. She must be far away—in some distant part of the City. Or maybe not even in the City at all.

He turned, following the direction of the sound. All of a sudden, he realized his error. She wasn't far away at all! Her heartbeat was so faint for a very different reason.

Promi sprinted down the street and turned into a small alley. Right in front of him lay Atlanta, bleeding steadily through the apron wrapped around her torso. Kneeling by her side were Shangri, Plato, and Morey, their faces almost as ashen as her own.

"Promi!" cried Shangri, her face stained with tears. "Ye got my prayer!"

He rushed over, kneeled beside Atlanta, and asked, "What happened?"

"Stabbed," said Shangri bitterly. "In the back."

Promi's face contorted as he gently lifted Atlanta's head. Listening to the inner workings of her injured body, he traced the damage to her muscles, bones, and organs. One lung had been punctured, and was swiftly filling with blood. The back of her heart had also been torn—so badly that the organ was failing fast. In less than a minute, he could tell, she would perish.

The life I care most about, he told himself in a panic. *The person I love more than any other.*

Somehow sensing his presence, Atlanta opened her eyes. Through the fog of her vision, she looked up at Promi, recognized him, and said weakly, "You . . . came back."

He nodded, feeling his own heart slamming against his ribs. "But not," he said despite his tightened throat, "to say good-bye."

She drew a ragged breath. "Someday, maybe . . . I'll see you . . . in the spirit realm."

"No, Atlanta! Not every person's spirit goes to the spirit realm.

Some are much more needed right down here, so they stay on Earth. And some who go to the spirit realm take ages and ages to arrive—longer than I want to wait!"

He shook his head, then added, "Besides, when your time to die comes, it shouldn't be like this! You have lots more living to do."

Pulling her face close, he whispered, "And when that time finally does come . . . I want to be right there to die with you."

As he said those words, an idea struck him. There was, perhaps, a way to save her!

Suddenly realizing what he was going to do, Atlanta's eyes widened. "No, Promi. Don't!"

Gathering what strength remained within her, she said, "Don't use your immortal power . . . to save me. Use it to save this island! This world! That monster—Promi, it's going to destroy Atlantis! And then . . . the rest of the world will get destroyed by its winged *offspring*."

"Offspring!" Promi exclaimed, aghast. In a flash, he understood Narkazan's boast of *something that will swiftly destroy any mortal foes.*

"But—" he protested. "It's *you* I want to save! Before . . ."

Her gaze caressed him. "I know, I know. But please . . . if you truly care about me . . . then help our world. All of it! Or so many creatures will die—people, faeries . . . even . . ."

She swallowed. "Even the young unicorn. Her name . . . is Myala."

Through the lump in his throat, Promi asked, "What if the only way to save the world is by destroying Atlantis? Our island, our home?"

"Then you should do it, Promi. Now!" she urged. "Before it's too late and the offspring take flight!"

He shook his head. "But what if that," he whispered hoarsely, "also destroys *you*?"

"Do it . . . anyway."

Turning to Shangri, Promi said, "There might be a way to stop that monster and its offspring. But it puts you—all of you—in great danger. You might not survive. Maybe *none* of you will survive."

Shangri clapped her hands together. "Do it!"

"Yes," agreed Plato. "If that's what it takes."

Morey, scowling, nodded.

Still cradling Atlanta's head in his hands, Promi said, "I'm going to try."

Her eyes brightened slightly.

"But listen," he added sternly. "Don't you dare go and die before I'm done."

She gave a weak nod.

Promi closed his eyes. He focused all his awareness on one essential truth: *For the mortal world to survive, Atlantis could not.*

His jaw clenched. To stop that monster, to end all this evil . . . he would need to destroy the very island he'd created. And if anything good about Atlantis was going to have some chance to survive—then the rest of Atlantis would have to be destroyed.

He knew it was crazy to try such a thing. He knew it might not even work. But he also knew that it was his only hope of ending all the evil he'd brought here . . . and possibly saving the lives of those he loved.

Feeling increasingly hot under his tunic, he remembered the mark over his heart. And he realized that if his idea really did work, then the last line of the Prophecy would take on a whole new meaning. *The end of all magic* would ultimately mean the end of the most magical place on Earth.

A resounding roar shook the buildings all around them. Then it came again—closer and angrier than before.

"The monster!" cried Shangri, her whole body shaking. "He's coming this way again!"

Promi concentrated hard, drawing on all his power, as well as all the power of the Starstone. He stretched his thoughts beyond the small alley where Atlanta lay dying, beyond the rampaging monster nearby, beyond the borders of the City. His thoughts soared past the sheer cliffs where ocean waves crashed, beyond the shallows where kelp stalks swayed rhythmically, beyond the currents that surged far beneath the surface of the sea.

All the way to the ocean's deepest waters. The place where he might find the most ancient goddess of the sea—O Washowoe-myra.

Once again, great goddess, I call on you. Though I am so small and you are so vast . . . please hear my plea!

Silence ensued, broken only by the rhythmic surging of the sea.

Finally, out of the depths, a voice arose. A voice that rolled like the endless waves and carried wisdom deeper than any abyss.

"I hear your plea, Prometheus, *swisssshhhhh*. Your voice is magnified by the Starstone, *swisssshhhhh*, as well as by the deeds you have done in the spirit realm."

At the distant edge of his hearing, Promi thought he heard the monster roar again. From even closer this time.

Great goddess, he said urgently, *I am calling for your help. At once! To destroy this island—to drown it and the monster and its offspring—under one enormous wave. Your most powerful wave.*

Currents stirred in the depths, carrying the reply.

"*Swisssshhhhh.* So you would have me destroy what was only just created? With all its wonders, all its marvels?"

Yes, great goddess. I would.

"Alas, *swisssshhhhh*, I cannot do that for anyone."

But you must! Promi cried. *I beg you, please. You must do this!*

Another pause . . . as waves pulsed, breaking on some faraway shore. At long last, the goddess spoke again.

"I was starting to say, *swisssshhhh*, that I cannot do what you ask for anyone—except you, Prometheus. You were this island's creator. So only you, *swisssshhhh*, can be its destroyer."

Thank you, great goddess, thank you!

"Prepare, *swisssshhhh*, for what comes next."

Promi started to say one more thing—but a terrible roar nearby jolted him back to the alley with Atlanta and the others. He opened his eyes. And he saw, moving down the larger street beyond the alley, the shadow of an enormous beast . . . coming steadily closer.

"The monster!" cried Shangri.

Plato reached for her hand, hoping to calm her, though he looked no less terrified. Beside them, Morey's burly form shuddered from head to toe.

Promi glanced down at Atlanta. He bit his lip, seeing that her eyes had closed. "Atlanta . . . ," he moaned.

She opened her eyes, though only a little, as if her eyelids were just too heavy to lift. Yet she still had enough strength to ask, "The monster . . . is it—"

A sudden, violent tremor cut her off. From deep below them, at the very roots of the island, the sea floor ruptured. More tremors followed, each one more powerful than the last.

The monster itself came into view. Sniffing the air vigorously, it halted outside the alley, drooling yellow slime. It roared, shaking the cobblestones beneath its hulking mass. With all it had devoured, its body had swollen even larger than before.

Suddenly—it saw them. Lurching forward, it smashed the building on one side of the alley as it bore down on its prey.

Promi kept his gaze focused on Atlanta, just as she kept looking up at him. Shangri squeezed Plato's hand. Morey held his breath.

The monster crashed toward them, knocking down mud-brick walls. With another roar, it opened its cavernous mouth, preparing to shoot its deadly tongue at its prey. The tongue rose out of the gurgling slime and then—

The most violent tremor yet rocked Atlantis. Buildings crumpled and streets burst apart. A huge crevasse opened right under the monster, swallowing it whole.

The monster's roar continued. But it grew quieter and quieter . . . until, at last, it ceased.

"We're safe!" cried Shangri. "The monster's no more!"

Plato and Morey hugged Shangri then hugged each other. Together, they celebrated, dancing with Shangri, shouting with joy.

Yet Promi hardly heard them. Still focusing on Atlanta, he was busy preparing himself for one last feat. If, somehow, it worked, it might save the life of a single person—the one dearest to his heart. Precious few seconds remained.

Although it meant making a great sacrifice, he knew that it was the only hope of saving Atlanta. And what he would lose seemed small indeed compared to what would be gained if he succeeded.

He paused, sending a quick prayer to his devoted sister in the spirit realm. *Forgive me, Jaladay, for what I'm about to do. Maybe someday . . . I will join you again.*

"By the gods and goddesses," he cried, raising his voice to the skies.

Immediately, his friends stopped their celebrations. They stiffened like statues, watching and waiting for what Promi would say next.

"From this moment onward," he declared, "I renounce forever my immortal life! Willingly, I part with all its powers and delights. All I ask . . ."

He paused, trembling, as he held Atlanta's head in his hands.

"All I ask is that you spare the life of this one mortal. This one person. This . . ."

A tear ran down his cheek, and he looked down on Atlanta's face. Her eyes closed, fluttered one last time, then fell completely still.

His voice the barest whisper, Promi said, "This woman I love."

The teardrop fell from his cheek onto Atlanta's chin. Yet she didn't move again. Nor did the others in the alley. For all of them knew the bitter truth.

Atlanta had died.

CHAPTER 33

Tidal Wave

Another tremor rocked the City, opening up a huge crevasse that snaked right through the middle of the market square. Several buildings crashed down, while fires engulfed many of those still standing. The crevasse widened, swallowing vehicles, walls, and bodies.

Out at the river gorge, the fabled Bridge to Nowhere wobbled precariously. All at once, it crumpled and splintered. The entire structure, prayer leaves and all, spilled down into the raging river below. The last few leaves, and the impassioned prayers they held, drifted slowly downward until they disappeared into the billowing mist.

On the island's northern cliffs, seabirds suddenly took flight. Pelicans, sandpipers, cranes, flamingos, puffins, terns, seagulls, and more leaped into the air, leaving their nests behind. Even a newly hatched albatross, carried by its devoted mother, joined the throng.

The birds wheeled around the island's north side, screeching and honking and crying. So many birds joined the flock that they blotted out the sun, casting a dark shadow over the coastline of Atlantis.

The enormous flock flew eastward, heading for the faraway continents of Europe, Asia, and Africa. Every last bird had decided to brave the perilous seas on that lengthy journey, a journey they might not survive. For they had seen what no other creatures on Atlantis had yet noticed—a sight that commanded, *Flee now, if you can!*

Rolling rapidly toward the island from the deepest waters of the north came a single, gigantic wave. Triggered by the eruptions on the sea floor, it swelled larger by the second, obscuring the horizon and much of the sky. Like a liquid mountain range, the tidal wave sped toward Atlantis.

Meanwhile, in the alley near the demolished temple, the companions remained silent. Lost in grief for Atlanta, Promi and the others had nothing at all to say. And no desire to move. Even if they had been aware of all the tumult on the island, and the growing dangers they faced, they wouldn't have budged.

Cradling Atlanta's head, Promi gently kissed her forehead. Already, her skin felt cold to the touch of his lips. "I'm sorry," he whispered.

Unable to look at her dead body any longer, he turned away. Dejected, he peered at the cobblestones.

"Don't be sorry," said a familiar voice.

"Atlanta!" shouted Promi, hugging her head tightly. "You're alive!"

Shangri batted him happily on the shoulder. "Give her some room to breathe, Promi! Ye jest saved her, so best not to smother her!"

As she, Plato, and Morey all burst out laughing, Promi sat back and studied the blue-green eyes gazing up at him. They told him all he needed to know, for they shone with the vitality of someone he knew well. Someone he really thought he'd lost.

Slowly, Atlanta sat up. Pulling off the apron, she winced at all the blood that stained it. Then, lifting her arms and twisting at the waist, she peered at Promi, astonished.

"The wound," she said incredulously. "It's gone! I can't feel anything wrong."

Shangri smiled and indicated Promi. "A gift fer you from yer friend there."

Atlanta reached for Promi's hands. Together, they stood. Scrutinizing him closely, she asked a heartfelt question.

"What," she demanded, "did you sacrifice to save me?"

"Oh, nothing much," he said in a carefree tone.

"What?"

"Just . . . my immortality."

Stunned, she caught her breath. "Your *what?*"

"Immortality." He shrugged his shoulders. "Easy come, easy go."

Atlanta threw her arms around his neck and hugged him hard. "You are the most crazy, idiotic, foolish person I've ever met."

Looking him right in the eyes, she added, "And you're also the most wonderful person I've ever met."

"So," asked Promi, "that means you'll keep me around?"

"Well," she answered with a grin, "since you can't go back now to the spirit realm, I guess I'm stuck with you."

"That's good. Because, Atlanta . . ." His expression turned serious. "My place is right here with you. Whatever happens."

She cocked her head quizzically. "And why is that?"

"Because I want to!"

"And why," she repeated, "is that?"

"Because . . . I, well, I . . ."

"Yes?"

"I really love you!" he exclaimed.

Atlanta nodded, smiling. "Ah . . . *now* I understand." She shot a wink at Shangri, then added, "Sometimes I can be a bit slow."

"Not likely," he replied with a smirk. "But sometimes you'll slow down enough that I can catch up with you."

"Fair enough. Now what—"

"Look there!" shouted Morey. He pointed with concern at the sky, where thousands upon thousands of birds were massing in one enormous flock.

Atlanta stiffened. "Birds wouldn't do that—unless . . ."

Grabbing Promi by the arm, she ran with him down the alley, followed closely by the others. Stepping carefully around the crevasse that had swallowed the monster, they stood in the middle of the wide street. Then, all at once, they saw something that froze their hearts.

Through a gap in the ruins of some collapsed buildings, they saw a massive wall of water, rising higher as it sped across the sea toward them. Only a few moments remained before it would strike the island.

A tidal wave.

A certain end to everyone and everything on Atlantis.

"*A terrible day and night of destruction*," said Atlanta, recalling the grim prophecy.

She turned to face Promi. "At least we'll die together." Squeezing his hand, she added, "I just wish we'd had more time."

Glumly, she touched the collar of her robe, the favorite perch of a certain faery. "And I also wish I could have said good-bye to Quiggley."

"Wait," urged Promi. "There still might be a way to escape! If only we had a boat of some kind . . ."

"Nobody in this city has a boat," Plato commented, running a hand through his scraggly hair. "There's no port, and with all the cliffs, no place to get in or out of the water. Unless, of course, you have some help from the gods, as my ship did."

Shangri gave Promi a knowing look.

"Wait!" exclaimed Morey. "Ye jest gave me an idea—maybe the idea we need."

The baker cast a worried glance at the oncoming wave, which now rose so far above the horizon that it looked like an immense blue island—albeit an island bearing down on them rapidly. "Come on! I'll show ye!"

CHAPTER 34

One Great Story

M orey led them through twisting streets and alleys to the other side of the City. Everywhere, they passed sheer devastation—toppled buildings, deep crevasses, and piles of smoldering rubble. Very few people remained, which was understandable after all the tremors and the monster's violent chaos—and those people were either grieving inconsolably or wandering the streets in shock.

Taking care to avoid all the yawning crevasses, raging fires, and crumbling structures, the baker took them to the City's old outer wall. Though it had been built many centuries earlier, most of its stones and archways remained intact. Promi glanced beyond the wall at the grassy knoll crowned by an old cedar tree, the very place where he'd sat to eat the smackberry pie he'd stolen from right under the nose of the Divine Monk and the temple entourage.

So much has happened since then, he told himself. With a glance at Atlanta, he added, *And she is the best part.*

"Where are ye leadin' us, Papa?" Shangri called to the baker as he took them through an archway and onto a grassy path. "We don't have much time before that wave comes smashin' down!"

"I know, sugarcake," he replied, using his sleeve to mop the perspiration off his brow. "We're gettin' close now."

"But where are we headin'?" she pressed.

Panting from exertion, the burly man explained as he took them down the path, "Back in me early days, before ye came along, I used to deliver me own pastries. An' in those days, I'd take whatever business I could get."

Hooking her arm in his, she said affectionately, "Before yer pastries became famously the best eatin' around."

"No," he replied with a wink. "Before the most winnin' delivery girl *ever* started to help me."

"I believe that version," said Plato, who was right behind them.

"So do I," said both Atlanta and Promi in unison.

Shangri, blushing almost the color of her hair, urged her father, "Get on with yer answer, now. Where in the name o' sweetness are ye takin' us?"

Morey veered off the grassy path to an old, rutted gulley that might long ago have been some sort of trail. Yet it looked as if nobody had gone this way for many years. Trying not to stumble as he hurried, the baker continued to explain.

"One o' me first customers was an old fellow who lived down here, all by himself, at the very bottom. Named Rosso. Rarely came into town, since he'd made himself a comfy nest down under the cliffs."

The trail dropped steeply, winding down through loose rocks and overhangs. As they swung out toward the sea, the group had a wide view of the immense ocean—and the gargantuan tidal wave speeding toward Atlantis.

"This better work," said Promi worriedly. "Why do you want us to see Rosso's nest?"

"Because, lad," said Morey. He smacked his lips, as if he'd just tasted a well-baked pastry. "That nest o' his was a *boat*."

Shangri brightened, hopping over a washed-out section of the trail. "How big, Papa?"

"I don't recall. But ye'll soon see fer yerself."

Picking their way down the slope, they passed an abandoned row of birds' nests on a ledge. Now they were almost down to a small cove where water lapped rhythmically on the rocks. In the distance, the enormous wave gained both size and speed. For the first time, they heard the faint but swelling roar of its approach.

Morey led them around a bend by a huge boulder. Abruptly, he froze. The others bumped into his back, then looked beyond the boulder to see what had halted him.

There lay Rosso's boat. But it was clearly—

"Too small!" exclaimed Plato. "It can't possibly hold us."

Morey walked over and hefted the small boat, which had been protected from the full force of storms by the surrounding rocks. "Looks solid enough," he said. Spying a weathered pair of oars beside it, he nodded. "Them, too."

Facing the group, he announced, "This boat might not be big enough fer all o' us. But it *is* big enough fer *some* o' us."

He swallowed, then gazed straight at Shangri. "Which be why . . . I'm goin' to stay here."

"Papa, no!" She stepped over to him. "Yer brave to offer that, Papa . . . but ye jest can't!"

He reached up and touched her cheek, brushing it with one

finger. "It's the right thing to do, sugarcake. An' if yer lovin' ma were here . . . she'd agree."

"Papa . . ." No more words came to Shangri, just tears.

Plato frowned. "Morey," he asked, "are you really sure about this?"

The baker forced a small laugh. "I am, lad. Why, with all me weight, that boat would sink straightaway!"

Lovingly, he gazed at his daughter. "Besides . . . I've got some cinnamon buns back in the oven. An' I'll be needin' to look after 'em."

"Papa," she said softly, taking his plump hand in her own. With a glance at Plato, who nodded, she placed her father's hand on her belly. "Ye deserve to know . . . I've got my own bun in the oven."

Morey's eyes grew misty, and he hugged her tight. "I'm so very glad fer ye both."

Plato moved to where he could face Promi and Atlanta, as well as Shangri and her father. "I found something just now."

"What?" they all asked.

"I have found," he declared, straightening his back, "*my one great story.*"

"Ye did?" asked Shangri.

"Yes. The story of this island! The story of Atlantis."

Pointing at the boat, he continued, "If we survive our journey, I will tell that story with all the power I have. And I'll tell it with such passion, such clarity, that it will spread all around the world."

"People will always remember the name Plato," said Shangri proudly.

"More important than that," the young bard replied, "they will always remember the name *Atlantis.*"

Promi nodded, pleased. "People everywhere will hear your tale. They will never forget all the beauty, wonder, and greatness—as well as all the greed and sorrow—that belonged to Atlantis."

"And they also won't forget," added Atlanta, "that for a brief and beautiful time . . . it was the most magical place on Earth."

"And also," Promi said with a grin at Shangri, "the place with the most delicious cinnamon buns."

She started to smile—but a shadow suddenly fell over the cove and all of them. Looking out to sea, they realized with a jolt that the great wave had grown so tall it was now shading them. It swelled every second as they watched, growing in size as well as power.

"We don't have long left," said Shangri anxiously.

"And," Plato observed, "we have another problem." Pointing at the little rowboat, he said gravely, "It's not even big enough for the four of us. That thing will hold two people, maybe three at the most."

Everyone, looking at the boat, nodded sadly.

"But not," added Morey, "a third one as big as meself." Turning to Atlanta and Promi, he declared, "One of ye should leave in the boat. While ye still can."

The young couple faced each other. Clearing his throat, Promi started to speak—when Atlanta cut him off.

"I'm not going without you," she declared firmly.

"And I'm not going without *you*," he replied just as firmly.

For several seconds, they stood looking at each other. Meanwhile, the shadow on the cove darkened. A growing roar swelled off the coast.

Finally, Promi nodded. "Well then," he said, "it's settled."

"Right," agreed Atlanta.

"*What's* settled?" demanded Shangri. "Which one of ye will come with us?"

"Neither of us," Promi answered. Standing beside Atlanta, he wrapped his arm around her shoulder. "We're both staying."

"Are ye sure? I'm jest certain we could take a third passenger."

"Totally sure," said Atlanta, watching Shangri with clear eyes. "You must go, my friend. You'll be taking our love with you."

"And also this," declared Promi. Striding over to Shangri, he reached into his tunic pocket and pulled out the Starstone.

She gasped, gazing at the crystal that seemed so alive it almost pulsed like a beating heart. "The Starstone? But that's—"

"The most magical object in the world," finished Promi. He glanced overhead at the darkening sky above. "In *any* world, actually."

Placing it in Shangri's hand, he reminded her, "Much of the magic of Atlantis came from the powers of this crystal, which magnified all nature's beauty around it."

Atlanta stepped forward and said to Shangri, "Maybe you will find a new way to use its power. To keep alive the magic of Atlantis."

"And to bring that magic," Shangri added, "to a whole new place."

"Yes," agreed Promi. "And here is one more thing that could be useful." From his pocket, he pulled the old recipe book that Shangri had given him, then handed it to Plato. "Use it as your journal, if you need a place to write. Or, if you prefer, just use it for the recipes! Some good desserts in there, I can promise."

"You would know," said Atlanta.

"Now wait, young folk," boomed Morey. "If yer gonna survive in some faraway land . . . ye'll be needin' more than magic an' recipes to live on."

He reached down to the belt that circled his prominent waist. Removing the buckle, he held it up so that its sapphires shone as blue as a summer sky. He tossed it to his daughter, who quickly put the jeweled buckle, as well as the Starstone, in her most secure pocket.

Approvingly, Promi said to the baker, "Nice belt buckle there. Where did you ever get it?"

Morey almost grinned. "Oh, I once sold someone a very pricey cinnamon bun."

"It was worth it," the young man replied.

Behind them, the roar of water grew much louder. They turned to see the mountainous wave, now blocking much of the sky, speeding toward Atlantis. Great white crests curled at its upper edge, while below the water's color deepened to darker than midnight.

The group traded frightened glances. Only seconds remained before the wave would strike!

"Quick!" shouted Promi. "Get the boat into the water!"

Hurriedly, they carried the rowboat to the water's edge. Shangri gave each of them a last hug, saving the longest one for her father. Then she and Plato climbed into the little craft.

Positioning the oars, the young bard started to row them out to sea. He pulled as hard as he could—for he, like everyone else, knew that the boat and its passengers might never survive the powerful wave.

CHAPTER 35

The Last Passenger

W ait!" Atlanta suddenly shouted. Her cry rang out, audible even over the din of the oncoming tidal wave.

Hearing her, Plato pulled up the oars in their small boat. Both he and Shangri peered at their friend, wondering why she'd shouted.

Atlanta, meanwhile, spun around to face the rocky cliff rising above them. For she'd felt a sudden rush of feeling—which told her unmistakably to stop the boat. And that feeling had come from a source she knew well and trusted completely.

"Quiggley!" Flying down over the cliff came the tiny faery with luminous blue wings. Zipping across the cove, he landed on her collar. His antennae quivered and she felt a rush of gratitude.

"I'm glad to see you, too," Atlanta said, yelling to be heard over the wave. "But we have only seconds left! Why did you want me to stop the boat?"

The faery pointed back toward the cliff. Bounding down the rocky trail came two graceful creatures whose prominent horns glowed with subtle radiance.

"Gryffion," called Atlanta to the elder unicorn. "And Myala!"

The young unicorn bounded over to Atlanta's side. Stopping abruptly, she tapped Atlanta's hand with the tip of her horn. Immediately, she planted her silver hooves and then leaped all the way across the shallows to the boat. She landed gracefully right beside Shangri.

Wide-eyed, Shangri could only say, "I thought we had room fer someone else. But I never thought it'd be a unicorn!"

"Not just any unicorn," declared Gryffion as he clomped to the water's edge. "She is *the future*."

The wave drew closer, towering high over the island. It sucked the shallows toward it, pulling the rowboat swiftly away from shore. But the wave seemed just about to smash down on top of the little craft, destroying it and its passengers along with everything else on Atlantis.

Instantly, a glowing halo emerged from the young unicorn's horn. It swiftly expanded into a luminous sphere that surrounded the whole boat. Strengthened by the power of the Starstone, Myala's magic enveloped the vessel and those it held.

Atlanta slid her hand into Promi's. "Will they survive?" she asked.

"With so much magic of Atlantis on board," he answered, "they have a good chance."

Side by side, they watched the glowing sphere grow smaller, a tiny point of light in the vast darkness of the surrounding sea.

Yet perhaps because of that darkness, the light glowed all the brighter.

Looking deep into Atlanta's eyes, Promi said, "And whatever happens next . . . we will be together."

Atlanta nodded. Then she felt something in her other hand—the hand touched by the unicorn's horn. Eagerly, she opened it. And she saw, resting on her palm, a lovely flower that had silver petals, a lavender center, and the rich aroma of the forest.

CHAPTER 36

The Most Magical Place

The tidal wave crashed over Atlantis. Sweeping away everything and everyone, the ocean smashed whatever civilization had existed. In a few brief seconds, the wave erased all signs of settlements, landscapes, and creatures. No mortal beings survived.

Before long, only deep blue waves, rolling endlessly, marked the spot where there had once been an island. An island that had been, for a time, the most magical place on Earth.